X

FISH ON A HOOK

A university lecturer turned river-watcher, international agents, deer poachers, a game-keeper's beautiful wife and a conference of top physicists, all in close proximity to the Dounreay Atomic Station, are the chief ingredients in a racy thriller.

FISH ON A HOOK

by

Paul MacTyre

HODDER AND STOUGHTON

DRIAR

*The characters in this book are entirely
imaginary and bear no relation to any
living person*

Copyright © 1963 by Paul MacTyre

*Printed by Northumberland Press Ltd., Gateshead and
bound by C. Tinling & Co., Liverpool, London and
Prescot, for Hodder & Stoughton Ltd., St. Paul's
House, Warwick Square, London, E.C.4*

CHAPTER ONE

ALASDAIR was thinking about going home when Johnnie
the hotel-keeper came into the bar and told him that MacAra
was in the office and wanting to see him. The men were coming in before the concert started in the hall across the road, and
the bar was filling up and beginning to get noisy. Soon the com-
bination of beer and whisky would be having its effect. There
would be arguments, bursts of quick talking, laughter with
depths of menace or ridicule in it that he could only guess at.
Uisdean from the garage was eyeing him already across the
length of the bar. Alasdair knew what Uisdean was trying to
do. He wanted Alasdair to suspect that he would be having a
go at the river before the night was out. No malice; just part
of the ritual of living in the strath. There was nothing simple
about the valley of the Blackwater and its people, thought
Alasdair, who knew perfectly well that Uisdean wouldn't
waste his time after salmon when there was a dance to go to.
The place was complex, the people more so; an incomer of a
year's standing, and only hired to watch the river and save its
salmon from the local experts, already he could catch something
of that complexity.

MacAra's message was a nuisance, for he had to get a meal
before going out on his evening patrol. Still, it might mean
more to drink. MacAra knew good whisky, and knew how to
get it—not the raw blends that were popular in the bar, but
malt whiskies so good that they were anonymous. It would be
worth going to the office for such a whisky, even if it meant
leaving the bar and walking round to the front door of the
hotel. There were no poachers there, only two stuffed eagles
and a monstrous trout, allegedly caught by a colonial bishop
ninety years back. Alasdair liked the eagles; they still stared

5

arrogantly at intrepid tourists with their unwinking eyes. The trout, though, had long since lost both eyes and tail, and he made Alasdair feel tired and down-at-heel. But whisky was whisky. Besides, he had to do what MacAra wanted, for he only held his job by the lawyer's courtesy.

He emptied his glass and went outside into the early evening. Across the road the hall door was open, and the children were beginning to go in. Women were straggling back up the road from Donnie's shop, while the determined ones waited grimly outside the bar for their menfolk. Probably ninety per cent of the population within a ten-mile radius was in Halmidary for the concert; with some surprise Alasdair realised that he knew almost all of them by sight—keepers in tweeds, shepherds with crooks and collie-dogs, the stationmaster and the garage owner, the schoolmistress and the doctor from Rhintraid at the foot of the strath, twelve miles away. It was the world he lived in, even though it wasn't his world—yet.

He walked along the front of the hotel, past the corrugated iron wing that housed the bar, and up to the battered front door with its faded paint, and the even more faded sign above. This was a Highland hotel, a hotel for fishermen and not for casual tourists, and it bore all the marks of the type—the depressed verandah with the wickerwork chairs and the rows of leering fish, the dark hallway, the air of comfortable neglect. He looked at it affectionately, and turned at the entrance to take in once again the little world of the strath.

The view was neither dramatic nor beautiful. A sparse fir plantation, a green field more full of rushes than grass, a single-track road with a scatter of houses along it, a station and a bridge bringing in the railway line—that was Halmidary. But, beyond, heather—infinity upon infinity of heather, flowing over low rolling hills, dipping down to the folds of a rock-studded river, and rising beyond to more hills and more again, with far away the blue spine of a great mountain, the high tops of Creag an Lochain. Southwards, the grey tarred road followed the sweep of the river valley; northwards, it climbed away from the water and turned on to a wide desolate moor. A narrow reddish-brown gravel track broke from the road and wandered up the near side of the valley, passing out of sight over the crest of a hill. Even now, on a June evening, with the sun slanting down from a clear sky, it was a land to respect and to fear.

He went into the hotel, and opened the door into the office. MacAra had the whisky organised already. He was sitting in a chair, his fingers tapping the sides of his glass. He looked at Alasdair straight—too straight. Alasdair took his time, pulling off his cap as slowly as he could without looking clumsy, trying not to be left standing, waiting for MacAra to ask him to sit down. The old man, it came to him, was anxious about something. It puzzled Alasdair. MacAra was never much worried about me before, he thought, even though he knows well enough that I've been thrown out of the university where he graduated God knows how many years ago. Not that respectability worried MacAra. He had drunk too much whisky with too many men, and pursued too many women successfully, to think much about his own reputation or anyone else's. He was rising seventy, and he could cast a long line, bring down a running stag, or kill a twisting ptarmigan better than most. He knew it too, and enjoyed it. His business—he was a lawyer in Rhintraid—was well enough run. He had an eye for trouble, and a genius, rare in his profession, for getting good work out of men who spent their time in the open air. Certainly, he was a competent estate factor, and the half-dozen proprietors for whom he ran the fishings, in addition to the shooting-forests, were well served. A spent old beast, perhaps; but Alasdair Macvartney, one-time lecturer in the University of Perth, and now river-watcher on the Blackwater, could think of many men he would less like to work for.

"Sit down, Alasdair. Are the fish over the falls yet?"

"Thank you, Mr. MacAra. No, I'm thinking it's early enough for them. They'll be waiting for a fresh spate to move them out of Loch Beannachd. There's been no fish caught above the Devil's Pool yet, and Wynrame was telling me this afternoon that he hasn't had a rod out on Craggan."

MacAra nodded. He knew it all already, of course, for he

had fished the Blackwater for fifty years himself. It was a good river. The spring salmon began to run in from the North Sea in February, and men paid good money to fish for them on the lower waters in the teeth of the cold east wind. Loch Beannachd, half-way upstream, held them through the late spring, and let the older enthusiasts sit in a boat and fish with greater comfort, if less accuracy. In the summer and autumn the inevitable Highland rains brought tumbling floods that made the headwaters above the Halmidary falls teem with urgent fish on their way to remote Loch Skiag and the spawning grounds under Creag an Lochain. Twenty miles of good fishing water, half-a-dozen lodges to divide it between them, and MacAra to look after it all. Pretentious lodges, like Craggan, three miles above Halmidary along the gravel track, built in the late nineteenth century, when deer and salmon had seemed an endless source of wealth; simple lodges, like Corrachan, four miles further upstream, where the Blackwater left Loch Skiag, a box of corrugated iron and wood, where the front door opened into the living room and every other room did the same. In his office in Rhintraid MacAra had an enormous map of the whole county on one wall; he knew it all like the back of his hand. Even the driest of Scots lawyers, with his feu-charters and his teinds, his eiks and his reversions, could never be far away from the land and those who lived by it if he had such a map before him. Alasdair, who had once upon a time made his living by giving carefully petrified lectures on field systems and the agricultural habits of twelfth-century Bavarians, felt a stab of envy. MacAra, lean, old, bleached, was a bigger man than he himself could ever be.

The door opened, and someone entered. Alasdair, his back to the door, couldn't see who it was, but MacAra could.

"Come away in, Duncan," he said. "This is Alasdair Macvartney, the watcher on the upper river. He covers everything from here to Loch Skiag. Alasdair, I want you to meet Mr. Duncan Gruar. His father is an old friend of mine, and he's come to help me in the office for a few months. I'm hoping he'll take some of the river work off my hands, so you'll be seeing a good deal of him, I expect. And he knows what a salmon rod's for, too."

Alasdair got up and turned round to face the newcomer. Gruar was another of the breed; that was the first impression. He wore tweeds and carried a deerstalker in his hand, his shoes were old and solid, he was smoking a comfortable-looking pipe. At first sight, a factor or a resident bonnet-laird, not a brand new fishing tenant from London or Boston. At second sight, rather more interesting. A slight man, but with heavy shoulders and a face that hadn't been dried out in any Edinburgh office. Unobtrusive, but not a man to be overlooked.

His voice confirmed the impression.

"I'm glad to meet you, Alasdair, and I'm looking forward to seeing this river of yours. Maybe you'll take me over it one of these days and show me the lies."

Alasdair liked him. He could enjoy a day on the river with him.

"Certainly, sir. You'll find me at my cottage most mornings. I'm usually out at the river from late afternoon on, but Mr. MacAra knows the way to get hold of me there."

"Good. One day soon, then, I hope," said Gruar.

MacAra poured out two more glasses of whisky and pushed them across the table. Alasdair sat down again, and took the offered glass. He watched Gruar take his. The malt was good, as Johnnie's special stock always was, and he wanted to see what Gruar made of it. Alasdair knew it of old, and enjoyed knowing it. He was pleased to see that Gruar took his time with it.

MacAra leaned back in his chair and lit a pipe.

"Well, Duncan, you've seen a bit of the strath already. I've been taking the chance, Alasdair, to show Mr. Gruar some of our local sights. I thought that Geare, the shepherd from Traligill, was going back to Ross-shire, but he's still here, I see. He's quite a load of whisky inside him tonight. Maybe his wife isn't all that sensible in wanting to get nearer the Dingwall shops. Tell me, though, have you seen Wynrame this afternoon?"

"Yes, Mr. MacAra. He and his wife were at the shop earlier on."

Alasdair didn't want to say any more. Mention of Wynrame, the Craggan keeper, always made him uneasy. He had never made up his mind why it should. Perhaps it was just that the square-faced keeper, with his absurd tow-coloured hair, seemed as much out of his natural environment in the strath as Alasdair felt himself. They met on the river often enough, for Alasdair's patrols took in the Craggan water. But they rarely said much to each other, and usually they were both ready to let it go at that. Wynrame was defensive, a man who concentrated too much, whose face was too blank, too shut-in, too anonymous. A good enough keeper within limits, according to the local gossip, though he didn't over-exert himself, but not a man whom anyone ever got to know. Obscurely Alasdair envied him for the capacity to stay out, for being able to hold the people of the strath at arm's length and keep them there—not because he couldn't bring them near enough, but because he didn't want to. But for all that, Alasdair didn't like him.

And then there was Wynrame's wife, dark, tense, disturbingly luxurious to the senses. Alasdair had met her—not often, but enough to be uneasily aware that he would like to know her better. It didn't do to think too much about that.

MacAra lingered on the subject.

"Wynrame's interesting, Duncan," he said. "He's the keeper at Craggan, as I told you. His father was an Orkneyman, but I've never been able to get him to talk much about himself. I don't know that he works very hard, and I wouldn't be surprised if Sir John Vaus got rid of him soon. But maybe it doesn't matter all that much if the Craggan keeper is lazy, seeing the lodge is always full of people who can't shoot and don't fish."

Gruar nodded. Information is passing, thought Alasdair. He wished he knew why. MacAra didn't usually open his mouth so wide, but here he was as good as telling Gruar that Wynrame was a fraud, and that Craggan was a place where other things mattered more than sport.

Certainly Craggan was unusual. In Victorian days, when reading parties were the vogue, Plato and St. Augustine had not been unknown in shooting lodges. Now the average sporting tenant was more likely to worry about the stock exchange prices, or the best market for his salmon. But Craggan had reverted to type. Sir John Vaus, the London banker whose father had married the last heiress of the old local proprietors, liked Craggan, and had intellectual aspirations. As a result, and to the exasperation of MacAra, the lodge normally housed a miscellaneous collection of figures from the university world and its fringes. Conference was the magic word. Craggan was a great place for conferences, and the salmon and the red deer flourished accordingly.

There were, however, conferences and conferences. There were the bogus conferences, whose members quite clearly knew that they were bogus. The people who attended these conferences came down to Halmidary to drink, to buy cigarettes, to ask for London newspapers that Donnie in the shop had too much sense to stock. They were tourists, nothing more, and they were fleeced accordingly.

Other conferences were different. Then the shutters went up at Craggan. The river was fished assiduously by anonymous men in tweeds, there were sudden bursts of road-mending, and it became impossible to go anywhere near the lodge without being questioned. On these occasions Johnnie at the hotel and Donnie at the shop waited in vain for customers, and the word went round the strath that something secret was happening again up at Craggan.

Alasdair knew a little more. It had been common talk amongst scientists at the University that Craggan was used for conferences about atomic physics; its nearness to Dounreay—less than thirty miles away over the Caithness border—was the attraction.

Did Gruar know all this? Alasdair looked at him. Probably he did know and if he didn't, MacAra would tell him in his own time.

Johnnie came into the office and sat down, his mild round

face expressionless. Alasdair wasn't deceived. Johnnie and his office were two of the same kind. The whisky might be buried under stacks of magazines, old calendars and trade circulars, but Johnnie always knew just how many bottles he had in stock. There were papers all over his desk, and he had a fine arrogance with impatient tradesmen and their charges, but his guests got good value. Like so many Highland hotel-keepers, he had been a gamekeeper in his time, and he and MacAra were old cronies. The hotel was not over-comfortable, the guests were in imminent danger of death by fire in the tinder-dry buildings, but fishermen came back year after year and enjoyed themselves.

Johnnie's standards were not obvious, but they were definite. The office was always kept locked when he was out of it; only a few people, like MacAra, were allowed to use it. Again, Johnnie knew his position in the society of the strath, and he respected it. He knew what was going on, yet he never abused his knowledge. To MacAra he spoke freely on most things, but in front of some people he said nothing at all. Thus, he never spoke much to Ian the barman, or the local policeman, Constable Thomson at Rhintraid. The reason, Alasdair suspected, was the same in each case. Ian was from Inverness, a town grown too modern and glittering for Johnnie's liking. Thomson was from Glasgow, and few people thought that he would stay long at Rhintraid. Each was an outsider, and each in his own way had a special position. Johnnie would never interfere with any job that the policeman had to do, but he didn't go out of his way to tell him things. And Ian was well placed to lend a helping hand to anyone from outside who wanted to get local information. Johnnie, in fact, knew how to live in the strath.

The hotel-keeper picked up a glass and filled it.

"There's an awful rush on the bar tonight," he complained. "I'm thinking I'll have to go and give Ian a hand before we're through. It's this concert and the dance after it that's the trouble. And these people from Craggan are in the lounge to-night, calling for drinks every five minutes."

"You'll be doing well enough with the bar, though, Johnnie," MacAra said. "It's been a fine day, too."

"Indeed yes, Mr. MacAra, though I'm thinking the rain is not far away."

"No harm if it is. Alasdair here will be glad enough to see his fish moving up a bit faster."

"The gentleman who's taken the Kinloch water hasn't had a chance yet, and it would be a pity if he had a blank month altogether," said Johnnie. "I dare say you would be pleased yourself if the deer could get away from the poachers with no more help than a night's rain."

Dry weather was the great danger time with the salmon poachers. If once the fish got into the river, and then the level fell, they were trapped in the pools, waiting for the next spate to give them a chance to move on towards the spawning grounds. Only in fresh, rising water would the salmon keep going upstream; when the river was low they sulked and refused to budge, and then the poachers got their chance. A spate would certainly suit Alasdair soon. Not that he had a great deal of trouble—certainly far less than his predecessors had had before Parliament had stiffened the laws against poaching. But there was always the odd case, and a low river was a temptation.

Deer were none of Alasdair's business. He was paid to watch the river, and it was the gamekeepers and the police who had to deal with the local specialists with their rifles. Before the Deer Act had been passed there had been more serious troubles, and hard war against the motor gangs. That had been an awkward, dirty business, chasing men who used shotguns against calving hinds, and who made their money by shipping the ruined carcasses south to the cities. Things were quieter now in most parts of the Highlands.

Not in the Blackwater strath, though. That, Alasdair knew, was the point of Johnnie's remark. The strath had always been an attractive target, for the road ran up its whole length from Rhintraid to Halmidary, and then swung away north over the moors to Invermudale, giving a convenient second escape hole.

A cul-de-sac was what the poachers liked least, and as a result the strath had suffered.

Obviously it had suffered again, though Alasdair had heard nothing of it. The recollection was rankling with MacAra.

"So you've heard about that, Johnnie," he said. "I didn't think it would be kept quiet for long, after the police car was on the road last night. That McGlashan crew got three hinds near Kinloch. We found the heads, and a good deal of blood beside the road. Geordie, the keeper at Kinloch, thinks there may have been some more wounded, and he's been out on the hill today trying to find them and finish them off."

"Who's McGlashan?" Gruar asked.

"He's from Perth," MacAra replied. "I think he's a scrap dealer or something like that. Anyway, he used to organise a lot of the poaching in the north before the Act went through. You know the sort of thing—old American cars with swivelling spotlights, shotguns, and a bunch of calving hinds down on the flats beside the river as the easiest target."

"Ach, it used to make me sick, Mr. Gruar," said Johnnie. "You won't find many people around here who like that sort of thing. The forests aren't kept as they used to be, and now and then the odd beast ends up where it shouldn't, but that doesn't mean that we're wanting these damned poachers from the south about here. I'm wondering, too, just why they're still at it. It's a risky business now, with the new fines and the chance of having the car confiscated."

MacAra was silent for a moment. Alasdair saw him glance quickly at Gruar before he spoke.

"I'd like to know that myself, Johnnie. It was McGlashan all right last night. The Ross-shire police saw him in the afternoon on his way up. Then Constable Thomson saw the car again at Rhintraid bridge as they were getting away, but they managed to dodge the patrol car somewhere along the coast road. No doubt about it, McGlashan again. But why does he keep on pestering us? There are a dozen other places he could try, yet he's been up the strath five times this year."

There was a silence when MacAra had finished. Alasdair

picked up his glass and drained it, watching the blue smoke from MacAra's pipe curl in the sunlight from the one small window. The unanswered question hung heavy in the air.

A bell rang. Johnnie lumbered to his feet.

"That'll be the Craggan people in the lounge," he said. "I'd better go and get their drinks for them."

"Who are they?" MacAra asked.

"I wouldn't be knowing. They haven't been here before. There's a couple, and two older men—one tall chap with white hair and an Inverness cape, a thing I haven't seen in the strath since the old Marquis died."

Alasdair stiffened. He knew one man with white hair who wore an Inverness cape, and that man was the President of the University of Perth. There couldn't be anyone else who wore a cape in June, who dressed for the Highlands regardless of the season or the weather. Alasdair put his glass down carefully. This was a time for keeping out of sight. Not that he wished the President any ill. He hadn't left Perth because President Crossrig had wanted him to go. It had looked like that, but he knew himself that he had really left because he had been headstrong and opinionated—and because he had done certain things. Still, Alexander Crossrig could have kept him if he had wanted to, could have stopped pressure being brought, could have stood up for a young man's right to be rude to his elders and betters. Crossrig hadn't wanted to. Probably he had been right. From the point of view of the University, people like Alasdair were nuisances, and unlikely to stop being nuisances. Father-figures made more sense—more academic sense, at least—if the children all behaved themselves. And that, Alasdair reminded himself, was just what he had not done.

So here was Crossrig in the Halmidary hotel, drinking—a physicist of international stature, and not a bad University President at that. But he stood for the past, and that hurt. Alasdair didn't want to see him.

His presence meant one thing, though. Crossrig would never have come to Craggan without a purpose. His annual holiday, fixed and inexorable, took him in August to the diminutive spa at Strathpeffer. Craggan in June was something different. What did it mean? Craggan was a place where conferences were held. Crossrig was an atomic physicist. It was long odds that there was going to be an atomic conference at Craggan soon—if it hadn't started already.

As the door closed behind Johnnie, MacAra reached for the bottle and refilled the three glasses.

"Old Donald, the keeper at Corrachan, is going to the hospital at Inverness tomorrow, Alasdair," the lawyer said.

"I knew he had to have an operation," Alasdair replied carefully. MacAra was tense again.

"Just so, just so. Now, I've got to find someone to fill his place for the next two months. There won't be any tenants in the lodge until August, when the owner is coming up, but I need someone to keep an eye on the forest, do some vermin killing and so on. Would you be willing to take on the job?"

The prospect was attractive. Up at Corrachan, where the road ended, he would be insulated from the world, free to do what he liked. Up at Corrachan he would escape from the strath, run into the ultimate hiding-hole where nobody who knew him could follow. That was the lure of the remote places, the places for those who couldn't take everyday life or who despised it too much. Not that most keepers fell into either category. As he knew them, they were simply normal people with enough stability and inner resources to stand the strain of the hard winter months, with possible isolation for weeks on end. They weren't concerned about taking the world or despising it. But for someone like himself the thought of two months at Corrachan in summer, when neither weather nor people presented any problems, was the most attractive of ivory towers. He had a long account to square with himself, an account that had been postponed for a whole year. And now that President Crossrig was at Craggan, Corrachan was the place to go.

"I could have a shot at it, certainly," he said slowly. "But what about the river watching? And don't expect me to be all that clever at shooting foxes, Mr. MacAra."

Behind his shoulder Alasdair could sense Gruar relaxing. He

heard the scrape of a match and the puff of a pipe. MacAra carefully avoided looking at Gruar. Again Alasdair caught a hint of tension, felt the surge of a deep, hidden current. Then it was gone.

"Good," MacAra said briskly. "I thought you'd help me out, Alasdair. I'll try to get hold of another watcher as soon as I can, though it won't be easy to find one at short notice. I thought we might make an arrangement that you took an occasional turn down as far as Halmidary, until a relief man turns up. Corrachan is really more important. There won't be much chance of any poaching next week, anyway. There's to be one of these conferences at Craggan."

The last words were too level, too unstressed. Suddenly Alasdair was aware that Gruar was linked in some way with Craggan and the conference. That made another complication, and he was sick of complications. But time enough to think about all that when he got to Corrachan.

"When do I go?" he asked.

"Tomorrow morning, if you can be ready in time. I'll send a lorry to take your stuff up to the lodge. Donald's wife is going off to stay with a niece in Inverness while he's in hospital, so you'll have the place to yourself. Can you milk a cow?"

The question was relevant, Alasdair realised after a second of blankness. Every keeper had his own cow, or maybe more. When the lodge was occupied he could supply milk and butter. He could sell off any calves in the same way as he sold the lambs from his small flock of sheep. In winter the milk and meat might be an invaluable bulwark if supplies became difficult. It was only reasonable that he should look after Donald's cow.

He grinned.

"Not as far as I know. But I'll try."

"Right. Wattie Jardine at Craggan farm could give you a hand if you're in any trouble. Come to that he could probably take the animal down to the farm if you want to come to Halmidary for a night or two. Do you want me to ask him?"

"Don't bother," Alasdair said. "I thought I'd go up as far

B

as Craggan tonight and take a look down the river. I'll be in at Wattie's for a cup of tea as usual, and I can see him there."

MacAra nodded. Wattie's farmhouse was often used as a reporting post, and he knew that Alasdair went about it a good deal when he was on his nightly patrols.

"Fine then, Alasdair." MacAra made no move to rise, but his tone was dismissive. Alasdair took the hint and stood up.

"Good night, Mr. MacAra," he said.

"Good night, Alasdair."

Gruar held the door open and followed Alasdair out into the hall.

"Maybe I'll come to the river with you tonight," he said. "How far are you going?"

"Just from Craggan farm down to the railway bridge, Mr. Gruar."

"Good. I'll come, then. When are you starting?"

Alasdair looked at his watch.

"It's 8.30 now. I must go home and eat, then cycle up to Craggan. I'll be at the farm at the back of 10."

"Good. I'll meet you there. The walk up will do me good, and I can pick up my car here when I get back."

He stood in the doorway of the office, in no hurry to go back inside. Alasdair felt uneasy. There was something artificial about the situation. Gruar was staring with unlikely interest at an improbable painting of a stag that hung on the staircase. Through the door Alasdair could see MacAra sitting motionless at the table. Both men, it came to him, were waiting for something.

The door of the lounge began to open. The Craggan party were leaving.

Alasdair moved quickly, forgetting that Gruar and MacAra could see him. He slipped through the door into the dining-room and stood still. The tablecloths and the cutlery, ready laid for the morning, glistened all round him. A sour smell of cabbage and pickles hovered in the air. Johnnie's food might not be bad, but it was not imaginative.

He listened. There were footsteps in the hall, then Crossrig's voice.

"Thank you. Good night. Professor Naverack, would you like to drive us back?"

There were more footsteps, and the sound of the front door closing, Alasdair took his time about moving. He had heard a name—Naverack, Evander Naverack, Winesack Professor of Entrepreneurial Ethics in the University of Perth. Alasdair didn't like him. Few people liked Naverack. Administration man, authority's yes-man, academic politician, idea-stealer without a single original thought of his own: he had been called all these, and worse things besides. It was all, Alasdair realised, a shade unfair. Naverack was hardly a professional academic. His chair was Winesack's endowment, and he himself—according to strong rumour—was Winesack's choice to fill it. Winesack—lord of a complex and only marginally respectable trading empire—had certainly enough knowledge of Naverack, for the Professor had spent several years inside the Winesack organisation, ending up as personal assistant and front-of-the-house man to the tycoon himself.

His appointment to Perth had been something of a scandal. But the University had needed Winesack's money, and so Naverack had been the price of two new laboratories. The new Professor's colleagues consoled themselves with the thought that Entrepreneurial Ethics was hardly likely to be a serious challenger to their own subjects; the more acid-minded were liable to add that a knowledge of entrepreneurial ethics did not necessarily imply a readiness to practise the highest brand of them.

So Naverack came to Perth. After a while some of his advantages began to appear. He could write a good, non-committal minute; he was a born systems man, an inveterate conference attender; he took over the management of the University's investment funds; above all, he made himself invaluable to Crossrig as an aide-de-camp and right-hand man. He was a tireless traveller, lecturing on the least provocation to any audience, advising industrial firms to provide money for the University, handling the press. His enemies, like Alasdair, believed that his income did not suffer as a result, but proof was difficult. Also, unpleasant stories about young men began to circulate. Again, though, nothing definite ever emerged.

Now Naverack was at Craggan. But why wasn't any of Alasdair's business. Suddenly and sharply, he wanted to get out into the open air, wanted to get away to Corrachan and his ivory tower. Crossrig had not fought to keep him at Perth, Naverack had done his best to get him out of the University. Being near them brought back too many memories—memories of a time when he had imagined that he knew everything and could say anything. Memories, too, of someone else. He shied away, and pulled the door open.

"See you later," Gruar said. He was still standing in the doorway of the office, his face a careful blank.

"Very good, Mr. Gruar," Alasdair said quickly, without looking at him. Then he was outside.

*   *   *

The sun was low in the west. Alasdair screwed his eyes up for a moment, shielding them with his hand. In the hall across the road a harsh nasal voice was cutting its way through a Gaelic song, with the audience bellowing all the choruses. Half a dozen sheepdogs, tethered outside the bar, were making their own contribution.

It was time to go up the hill to his cottage and cook a meal, if he was to be at Craggan on time. He walked down the hotel steps and out on to the road, glad to turn his back to the glare of the sunlight.

Wynrame was standing at the post-office corner. The train from the south had gone through, the Invermudale post-van had left, and the inevitable mail-time crowd had long since disappeared to the concert and the bar. Only Wynrame was left, one shoulder hunched against the locked door of the post-office.

The sun was striking straight along the road. Alasdair could see his own shadow bounding grotesquely forward with every step he took. With the glare to protect him, he looked at

Wynrame. The light caught the keeper, reducing him to a cardboard outline of a man. Motionless, he was a figure of obscure menace, his squatness accentuated by the tall doorway behind him, a deerstalker pulled down hard over his light-coloured hair.

Alasdair knew what was going to happen. As he passed Wynrame, he was going to nod. Wynrame was going to nod once in reply. Nothing strange in that. He had met people in the strath before, people whom he knew perfectly well, and though there was nobody else within miles they had passed with nothing more than the ghost of a nod. It was a quality of the place and the people, and Alasdair, an outsider who wanted desperately to lose himself in the strath, knew enough to respect it.

All the same, Wynrame was different. Wynrame was a keeper; he wore the same tweeds, served the same sort of master, did the same sort of work, as a dozen others. Short keepers, tall keepers, keepers who spent the winters getting drunk, keepers who tamed stags, keepers who played the great piobaireachds to empty hills, keepers who read Greek and Latin—keepers were a race, all different, yet basically all alike. All—except Wynrame.

What was wrong about Wynrame? It wasn't his dress—tweed plus-fours, a tattered Green Highlander in his cap, a leather game-bag on his shoulder, a solid-looking watch on a chain in his waistcoat. It wasn't that he was clearly not a native, for there were keepers in the strath who were Lowlanders, even one Englishman. It wasn't even his flat, controlled voice, with a hint of Canada behind it. As he drew nearer, Alasdair looked away. It was irrational, he knew, to distrust the man because he wasn't a native, when he was another of the same himself. But, for all that, the sight of Wynrame made him uneasy. The absurdly square face, the long, slightly crooked arms, the slate-grey eyes, as watchful as a weasel looking through a dyke, all made for a sense of disquiet. The air of detachment, of non-involvement, was unmistakable. And it was that, Alasdair realised, that he disliked most.

When it came, Wynrame's nod was almost a surprise. For a second, Alasdair tried to ignore it, then thought better of the attempt. But it was a relief to be past the post-office, past the squareness of Wynrame framed in the doorway.

Over the rise ahead a horn sounded. As Alasdair moved to the side of the road, a small green car came into sight from the direction of Rhintraid. The driver, he noticed, was Thomson the policeman. When he glanced back, thirty yards on, the car had stopped at the post-office, and Wynrame was getting into it.

CHAPTER TWO

By the time Alasdair had finished eating it was well after nine o'clock. The sun was still shining, but clouds were banking up to the south-west. A last look round the kitchen, an armful of peats for the fire, a full kettle beside the grate, and he was ready to go. If he was lucky, he would be home by midnight, and hot, sweet tea would be very welcome. If things went badly, as they always could, it might be first light before he got back.

He shut the door and walked through the derelict garden to the road. The clouds were closing in on the sun, and there was a suspicious softness in the wind. Rain before morning, and a spate inside three hours after that. He hoped he would be back home in bed before the weather broke.

For a moment he paused, from force of habit, and ran his field glasses over the strath. In the middle distance the Blackwater curved and looped, from the distant glimmer of Loch Beannachd away downstream up to the rocky ridge a couple of miles above the village that marked the falls. So far the salmon, baulked by the lack of water, had not passed the falls. They were lying in all the pools between Loch Beannachd and the Devil's Pool, just below the falls. Upstream he could catch a glimpse of another series of flats—the Craggan ground. The lodge itself was out of sight amongst birch woods, but a white building on the further, western bank was the farmhouse of Craggan, where he would meet Gruar in less than an hour's time. Behind it hills closed in, sweeping up to a long ridge; across the ridge, he knew, lay Loch Skiag and Corrachan. Black and infinitely remote in the fading light, the crest of Creag an Lochain cut into the northern sky. Nothing as high on this side of Greenland, only cold, deep waters, with unknown creatures in their depths, and uncharted, uncontrollable currents.

From the village below him came the sound of clapping and cheering. The concert was grinding along on its way. Round about 10.30 it would stop, the older people and the children would go home, and then, after half an hour, the dance would begin. But by then he would be three miles away. Not that he would have gone to the dance anyway. Too many blue suits, too many heavy boots, too many giggling, over-heated fisher-girls from the houses round the harbour at Rhintraid. Whatever sort of escape hole he needed, it wasn't that kind.

Out on the open moor on his right hand he could see a plume of smoke. The evening train from Caithness was on its way south. The sight of it stirred Alasdair into movement. He glanced at his watch—9.25. He would have to hurry to get to Craggan on time.

He walked quickly down the rough track to where his cycle lay at the edge of a clump of fir trees. By the time he had mounted, and bumped his way to the main road, the train was sliding down the long curve into Halmidary station. He reached the level-crossing gate at the end of the platform, just as the engine squealed to a halt with a hiss of steam. He dismounted, propped the cycle against the gates, and pulled out a packet of cigarettes. It would be five minutes before the gates would open, he knew. The train was too long for the platform, and the laborious ritual of double-stopping would have to take place. He stared at the restaurant car; a dejected pair of naval ratings stared back, glasses of lukewarm beer in their hands. Beyond the wheels of the coach he could see a car waiting on the far side of the gates.

Doors banged, a whistle blew, and at last the train was rattling and roaring up the incline to the bridge. Speculating on the policy that sent fewer and fewer trains along the single track line, and made them longer and heavier every year, Alasdair waited for John, the porter, to cycle up the platform and unlock the gates. He eyed the car beyond the gates idly, noticing with slight surprise that it was the green one he had

seen in the village earlier. This time there was no mistake.
Thomson the policeman was driving it.

The train rolled across the bridge, and swung away down
the strath towards Rhintraid and the sea. A strange porter,
hurrying more than John was accustomed to, opened the gates
and waved the car on. Thomson, his narrow face sharpened
by his peaked cap, nodded shortly as he started up and bounced
over the rails. Alasdair pushed his bike across and started on
the three mile ride to Craggan. Behind him an accordion began
to play in the hall. He put on speed.

The road twisted between the railway and the river, gradually
rising away from the water. For the first two miles it ran
through open moor. Then, on the crest of the rise, the railway
turned away northwards. Once over the ridge, and out of sight
of Halmidary, the birch woods began. Just inside them there
was a bridge, cutting across a narrow ravine. Alasdair slowed
down and stopped, one foot on the stone parapet.

Away from the village and the train, the silence was almost
absolute. Only the rustle of the birches in the south-west wind
broke its completeness. Beneath him, a hundred foot under the
bridge, he could see the glimmer of water. Upstream, the railway line, with its telegraph poles, stood out against the skyline.
Gradually his ears became attuned to the silence, and he began
to hear another sound. It was the distant roar of the falls, half
a mile away through the trees, below the point where the
stream beneath him joined the Blackwater.

He glanced at his watch. Ten minutes to go. Gruar must
have started in good time to walk up the road. The chances
were that he was already at the farm, and that meant that it
was time to be moving. He pushed the cycle away from
the bridge and started to pedal. High above his head a bird
flapped noisily out of the branches. In the silence it sounded
immense.

The road ran straight on through the trees, dropping towards
the river. The birches gave way to conifers, and his tyres hissed
over a carpet of pine needles. The light was beginning to go.
Three weeks more, and they would be at the longest day; after

that, the winter would begin to advance implacably behind all the warmth and the greenness.

Ahead there was a junction in the road. One track ran straight on. Tomorrow he would be using that track, for it led to Corrachan. But tonight to reach the farm he had to turn left, downhill, past Craggan lodge. A hundred yards beyond the fork, he slowed down and dismounted. He was on the edge of the lodge gardens, and the trees were beginning to give way to rhododendrons. If he left the road here, he could take a path behind the kennels and Wynrame's house, and keep out of sight of the lodge windows. The Victorian proprieties were a help; the outbuildings—stables, kennels, keeper's house— were all carefully screened from the lodge by shrubs. He might meet Wynrame, if the keeper had come home, but he was very unlikely to see Crossrig or Naverack. And just then he very much didn't want to see either of them.

Wynrame's house was shut, empty-looking. He hurried past. The gun dogs in the kennels were inside and asleep; another hurdle passed. Above the rhododendrons he could see the chimneys of the lodge. Ahead, there was less than another three hundred yards to the bridge. He was almost safe.

The woman was coming up the path towards him. Rounding a corner, he had to pull up short to avoid knocking into her. In the fading light, his first thought was of Mrs. Wynrame. Confused, half-excited, he was on the point of speaking when she began to laugh.

That pulled him up short. He knew the laugh, knew it far too well. Before he realised what he was doing, he had pitched the cycle aside and taken a step forward.

Erica Hakonson caught his hand just as it began to swing forward. Still laughing, she held it still for an instant. Then she pulled him towards her and before he could break away her mouth had fastened on his.

She began to shiver uncontrollably. That was enough. Alasdair pushed her off roughly and stood motionless, hands clenched at his side. Slowly his brain began to function again. This was the ultimate absurdity, the last blow at his precarious equilibrium. To meet her, of all people. Memories rushed in on him: memories of Erica, half-drunk, entirely provocative, man-hunting amongst the frightened intellectuals of the University; memories of hotel bedrooms, of Erica sober and demanding, shivering in that very same way as she lay in his arms.

Putting it all simply, he had gone to bed with the wife of a visiting American professor and had been found out. That was why he had left Perth. But it wasn't, after all, quite so simple. Erica must have slept with at least half a dozen of his colleagues during the year the Hakonsons had been at Perth. Nymphomania was always liable to be exacting. What Leif Hakonson —distinguished physicist from a U.S. Government research laboratory, his Norwegian origins imperfectly hidden under a New England veneer—made of it all was an open question. Alasdair, half-caught in the same trap, suspected that Hakonson was powerless to escape, didn't want to escape, didn't want to realise what sort of a woman his wife was. It wasn't a pretty thought.

Naverack knew. That had been the trouble. If only Naverack hadn't gone to the wrong hotel at the wrong time, the affair with Erica would have died its own death, and she would have moved on to the next victim. But Naverack had found out, and Naverack had his own scores to settle. Alasdair had opened his mouth too wide, had gone too far in attacking Naverack and his doings. Everyone had known that Naverack used his research students shamelessly and took all the credit for their work; everyone had known that a good deal of research money was somehow siphoned off to support Naverack's personal comfort. But only Alasdair had been fool enough to draw attention to it. And then he had let Naverack catch him in the one situation for which no explanation was of any use. In the circumstances, he had perhaps been lucky that he was only asked to resign. President Crossrig's views on morality set more store on what was seen than what was actually done, and so, as soon as Naverack had spoken to him, he had been anxious to get Alasdair away from Perth. Nothing had been said to anyone else. Hakonson had been told nothing. But in remarkably quick time Alasdair had found himself out of a job.

Now here was Erica at Craggan, her face as thin-drawn as ever, her instincts obviously no different. She stood in the shadow of a bush, her lips half-parted, her eyes fixed on him. He knew what she wanted; to begin where they had left off, to start the spiral all over again. And there was nothing he wanted less in the whole world.

Anger flooded over him. Was he never going to be able to escape from the past? Crossrig and Naverack at Craggan were enough. That Hakonson should have come across the Atlantic for the conference was unexpected, but not inexplicable. But that the man should have brought his wife to Craggan was the last straw.

Abruptly the anger exploded into action. He picked up the bicycle and started off down the path. As he walked past her he could see Erica's faultlessly blonde hair glinting in the last rays of the sun; there was a small white scar across the lobe of her left ear. Seeing the scar, being reminded at close quarters of her body, brought panic to reinforce the anger. He swung on his heel and looked straight at her.

"I don't mean to see you again if I can help it. Just remember that," he said.

Erica smiled and said nothing. She watched as he went down the hill between the rhododendron bushes. Gradually the smile faded.

*   *   *

Alasdair knocked once and pushed open the door of Craggan farmhouse. Leaving his coat and the field glass in the untidy little hall, he went into the kitchen.

Wattie Jardine was sitting in front of the fire, glaring incredulously at a farming paper lying open across his knees. Alasdair wasn't deceived. He knew Wattie for what he was—as good a judge and as good a breeder of Cheviot sheep as anyone north of Inverness, though he never admitted to anything but contempt for the land he farmed and the people he worked with. Alasdair had seen him in the ring at the great Lairg sales, where year after year he got top prices for his lambs, and where for a few hours he took on his real stature and held court for south-country farmers with voices as quiet as his own. A good man and a safe one, even if he refused to believe a word of what he saw in print.

Wattie looked up and nodded.

"You're here, Alasdair, I see. The kettle's on the fire. That man Gruar said you would be along tonight. I was half-expecting you anyway. Sit down and have a bit crack."

That was the nearest Wattie would get to a joke. The two of them were going to sit in companionable silence and ignore each other for the next half-hour—if Gruar let them alone, that was.

"Where's Mr. Gruar?" he asked.

"He came in half an hour ago, and went out to take a look round the lodge," Wattie said. "He ought to be back soon. The wife's out too. She went down to this concert in the village. I'm hoping the minister didn't see her go, for he was preaching pretty strong against it last Sunday."

Alasdair was inclined to back Mrs. Jardine, plump, sixtyish, as talkative as her husband was quiet, against the Rhintraid minister, a rigid Calvinist with strong views on the Sabbath. But he was glad that she was out; glad too that Gruar had gone wandering off into the gathering darkness. Now he had time to sit still and think, even if it was only for ten minutes. And he needed to think in peace.

He looked round the kitchen. It was as near as he was likely to get to a home. No Landseer stags, no family photographs, no tea-caddies with unflattering portraits of the Royal Family —only two framed pictures of very self-possessed rams, and a water colour of the triple folds of the Eildon hills, the enchanted hills of Thomas the Rhymer. The furniture was old and comfortable, the peat fire glowing and established. A place to relax in, a place to feel secure in. Small wonder that Wattie left it only once each year, to examine the Highland Show critically and revisit the Border country of his youth. Craggan farm was a good place to have roots in. Alasdair was unhappy for a moment, remembering that he was an outsider, remembering that he had lost his own roots.

He tried to review what had happened to him in the last four hours. It didn't amount to much in terms of action, but he sensed that it had enormous significance. There were currents all around him, and ahead, very close ahead, an unknown falls to be jumped. Like the salmon he guarded, he was trapped in tired, shallow water; like the salmon, he must be ready to run when the spate came.

Perhaps Corrachan was the chance. At Corrachan he could get away from Crossrig, from Naverack, above all from Erica. And there was more to Corrachan than that. As a river watcher he could never be more than an outsider. As a keeper, he could slip into the world of the strath on different terms. Go to Corrachan, lie quiet, keep out of the way of the conference at Craggan, out of the way of the disturbing Mrs. Wynrame, out of the way of Gruar, that soft-spoken man with the hint of hidden steel. That way he could avoid being involved again in the disastrous farce that his life at Perth had been. Moralising Presidents, peculating Professors, and man-eating American women; it was time to get away from them all.

Wattie turned over a page. What he saw on the next one seemed to please him even less than the last. He put down the paper and stared at the fire. After a while he pulled an ancient, battered pipe from his pocket, unscrewed the silver lid, and began to stuff it full with thick, black tobacco. Then he stopped and lifted his head. Somewhere outside a collie-dog was growling.

"Someone coming," Wattie said, and waited.

Over the sound of the river came the hollow rumble of feet on the wooden bridge. A pause, and then a knock on the door.

"Come in," Wattie called.

Gruar pushed the door open and came into the kitchen. Alasdair got to his feet.

"I'm back, you see, Mr. Jardine," Gruar said. "And I see Alasdair is here too."

"Just so, Mr. Gruar. Come in and sit down," Wattie said. Alasdair could sense the caution in his voice. Wattie took strangers on sufferance only.

Gruar dropped into a chair at the table and pulled out a packet of cigarettes. He glanced up at the tall pendulum clock hanging on the wall.

"Half past ten. When do you want to move, Alasdair?" he said.

"Whenever you like, Mr. Gruar. It'll be a bit darker in a quarter of an hour. Less chance of any poachers spotting us then. But I don't think there will be anyone out tonight."

"You might as well be waiting a while," Wattie said. "We could all be doing with a cup of tea. The wife will be back any minute, anyway."

Alasdair looked at Gruar, and waited for him to make the first move. But Gruar was quite prepared to stay. He stretched out his legs and looked at the fire. That made three of them. Alasdair would never have found three of his old colleagues who could have kept their mouths shut for as long. But he wasn't fooled. It was one thing to like Gruar; it was another to trust him completely.

The dog outside barked. Wattie got to his feet and poked the fire into life.

"That'll be the wife coming now. I didn't hear the truck."

Alasdair was suspicious at once. He didn't want to meet anyone else. It could be Wynrame, could even be someone from the lodge. When the door opened, he was on his feet already. He might have to get out quickly, just as he had had to hide in the hotel dining-room.

But it was Mrs. Jardine who came in. So he was caught off balance when, after a short pause, another figure followed her. It was Mrs. Wynrame.

Seeing her gave Alasdair a moment of cold panic, very different from that he had felt on meeting Erica. Wherever Ann Wynrame came from, it was not the strath, nor Orkney, nor any other part of Scotland. It was rumoured that she had lived abroad. Alasdair would have said himself that she had been born abroad, and had grown up there. Scots blood perhaps, but Scotland wasn't her native land. Dark, precise, her black hair drawn back from her face to give full play to eyes that took in far more than they gave out. The word was douce. He had known plenty of Highland women who looked douce, but in a way that made it clear that there was nothing behind the demure façade. Ann Wynrame was different; the devil alone could know what she was really like.

Alasdair caught himself wondering, saw himself standing back and watching her closely. Just what was she doing in the strath, he asked himself unbelievingly. She was out of place, far out of her natural environment. He could as readily imagine her in any of the genteel suburbs of Edinburgh, or amongst the professional wives at Perth. The thought came to him that Wynrame might be doing just what he was doing himself. Was the keeper a fugitive biochemist, or logician? But Wynrame wasn't the problem. The woman was the real mystery. What was she? Was her real name Chatterley—though Wynrame hardly seemed the kind of gamekeeper to fit into that picture?

It was, he realised uneasily, the beginning of involvement. And involvement was out—at least, that sort of involvement. He wanted to lose himself in the strath, not to chase Ann Wynrame. But the uneasiness remained. And Wattie was watching him. He sat down again, and listened to Mrs. Jardine, as she bustled about the kitchen. It was easy enough to listen, for Wattie's wife more than made up for her husband's silences.

"No, you didn't hear the truck," she told Wattie, her voice muffled as she rattled cups and saucers inside the tall wall cupboard. "It's in old Dr. MacCrossich's ditch, though not for the same reason as the one that used to put him there, I'd have you know. There was a big stone in the road, and we hit it. I've left the truck there for you to haul it out. Mrs. Wynrame was good enough to go and look for her husband to give us a hand, but he wasn't about. So we just walked on here together.

And you're not going to go away without a cup, Mrs. Wynrame, so take your coat off and wait two minutes. The kettle's singing already."

And that was that. Alasdair sat back and listened. For a while he felt a stab of anxiety as Gruar began to talk to Ann Wynrame. It soon passed, however. Gruar was treating her with his gloves on, making polite, unimportant noises. Another sign of involvement, this, to suspect that any other man who met her would automatically make a pass at her.

Tea, scones, home-baked cake, and Mrs. Jardine's flow of conversation. The wall clock struck eleven almost before Alasdair had realised that time was passing. At its sound Ann got to her feet.

"Time I went home. My husband may be back by now. Thank you very much for the tea, Mrs. Jardine."

"It's early yet. You're not going, surely?" Mrs. Jardine was insistent.

"I'm afraid I must. It's getting late."

"Oh well, if you must you must. Wattie will get his boots on and see you home. What's your husband doing?"

"Out looking for a fox somewhere in the woods. He was down in Halmidary seeing Thomson the policeman earlier, and then coming back through the woods. But your husband doesn't need to move. I can get home myself."

Alasdair waited for Gruar to speak, but Gruar said nothing. Wattie began to rise. Nothing for it but to make a move himself. One more step towards involvement.

"There's no need for you to go, Wattie. I can walk up with Mrs. Wynrame—that is, if Mr. Gruar doesn't mind waiting ten minutes."

"Of course, Alasdair." Gruar smiled briefly. Wattie shot a quick glance at his wife. She nodded.

"Very good then, Alasdair," said Wattie. "You could meet Mr. Gruar at the wire bridge and save a bit of time."

"Quite right. There's a sort of a bridge about three hundred yards down the river, Mr. Gruar. You can't miss it. I'll cut through the woods on the other bank and meet you there."

C

Gruar nodded agreement. Quickly Alasdair slipped into his raincoat and put the field glasses over his shoulder. By the time he was ready Ann was out into the yard, and Wattie was holding the door open for him.

"Good night, Wattie. And thank you. Oh, I nearly forgot. I'm going up to Corrachan tomorrow when Donald goes to the hospital. Could you perhaps look up and give me some instruction on dealing with the cow?"

Wattie laughed.

"That old bag. You'll have your hands full there. But I'm going round the ewes in the evening, and I can easy look in at Corrachan."

"Thanks."

"Good night, then, Alasdair. Come in the next time you're passing."

Then he was out in the half-dark with the woman beside him. His boots scraped on the gravel of the road, drowning the more precise sound of her shoes. Fifty yards to the bridge, a quarter of a mile up the winding path through the rhododendrons. He had an impulse to keep to the road and march past the big drawing-room windows of the lodge, but he drove it away. The path was the right way for a watcher and a keeper's wife, even if she was Ann Wynrame and doing things to his peace of mind. The hollow rumble of the planks as they came on to the bridge echoed what was going on inside his head.

"What do you find to do all night when you're on the river?" she asked.

"It's my job, Mrs. Wynrame, and that's about all there is to it."

"My name is Ann—Alasdair. Tell me, what are you doing up here tonight?"

The question sounded serious. But, bad though the light was, he got the impression that she was smiling.

"Routine. I'm going to Corrachan tomorrow, and I wanted to have a last look round."

"You're not looking for anything special?"

"No. Should I?"

She laughed softly.

"There's going to be another conference here, starting on Sunday. You know that, I suppose? I was just wondering about that man Gruar."

They rounded a bend in the path. He had met Erica there, less than an hour before. It seemed an infinity of time ago.

The rhododendrons closed in, and the dark with them. The path was narrow, and he had to follow close behind Ann to know where he was going. And so, when she stopped suddenly, he stumbled and pushed up against her. She caught his arm tightly and held him still.

"Look. There's somebody crossing the path ahead of us."

Alasdair looked. Was she making a fool of him? Was it Wynrame, ready to play the outraged husband? What sort of deep waters was he getting into? But he could see little—only a shadow, moving fast, slipping through the trees, going in the direction of the lodge. He listened and watched, but the shadow was gone, and there was nothing more to be seen.

Ann's breathing relaxed, and with it her grip on his arm, and irrelevantly he realised how short she must be. His arms tightened, and she pushed him away precisely and un-equivocally.

"Was that how you lost your last job? No, I'm sorry. I had no right to say that. Come on. I must get home."

Alasdair said nothing. He followed her through the trees, past the back of the kennels and up to her cottage. Along its gables rows of antlers stood out with ridiculous effrontery. Was his own head to go there too? Was Wynrame what he was because he had been cuckolded too often? No; it was his turn to retract. He had no right to think that—and all at once he knew that he wouldn't mind even if it was true.

Ann was douce again. She didn't look unhappy, and she didn't pull her hand away when he took hold of it.

"Good night. Thank you for coming with me. I hope you haven't been away from your job too long."

Then she had opened the door and was inside the house before he could open his mouth.

*   *   *

The bridge was a crazy contraption, no more than a foot wire and a hand wire along which it was possible to lurch sideways. It was a cheap means of communication, and innocuous in summer, when crossing was nothing worse than undignified. There could be days in January and February, though, with the winter spates lapping over the bottom wire, when a traverse called for steady nerves.

Alasdair saw the two supporting posts against the skyline as he came out of the trees a hundred and fifty yards away. It was appreciably darker now, and the clouds were heavy and ominous. Already he had felt an occasional fleck of rain against his face. Time to find Gruar and get the walk downstream to the Halmidary railway bridge over and done with before the rain came in earnest.

He walked out on to the level haugh, stumbling from time to time on the uneven tussocky grass. Then he stopped. Someone was crossing the bridge—or rather, two people, out of step and balance, sending the wires swinging wildly as they did so. Poachers? Possibly, but it wasn't very likely. If they were poachers, they were not very intelligent ones; no sense in risking a night on the river unless you went where the salmon were lying. More probably it was some of the lodge party. But it was his job to watch the river, and he had to find out who the men were. He moved forward again, keeping well bent and in the cover of the trees behind him.

As he got nearer he was able to make out more details. The two men were making heavy weather of the crossing. Once they had to stop until the wires steadied. Ahead, on the west bank, there was a darker patch against the heather that could be Gruar.

The two men were almost across now. The leader let go and dropped off the wire on to the bank. His companion was on the point of following him when a new figure appeared on the east bank, just beside the bridge post. This time Alasdair had no difficulty in recognising who it was—Wynrame, carrying a gun in the crook of his arm.

The keeper's call came clearly across the meadow.

"Wait a moment, whoever you are. I want a word with you."

There was a pause. Then the second man jumped down. A voice replied. It was President Crossrig.

"Yes, yes, what is it?"

Another pause, then the sound of boots splashing through the water. Wynrame wasn't waiting to use the bridge.

"Good evening, sir." It was Wynrame speaking this time. "Sorry I shouted. I couldn't make out who you were for a minute. We have to keep our eyes on the river these nights, just in case there are poachers about. I hope I didn't alarm you."

The man makes the right noises, Alasdair thought cynically. President Alexander Crossrig won't notice anything wrong. But I'd be prepared to bet that Wynrame is no more a real keeper than I am a real watcher.

The President was speaking again.

"Not at all, Wynrame. Professor Hakonson and I have been taking a stroll along the river, and we decided to cross this rather odd bridge of yours before turning back. I don't know if the Professor can poach a salmon, but I certainly wouldn't know how to begin."

So the second man was Hakonson. Alasdair stopped where he stood. Better to keep out of sight if possible. The chances were that neither Crossrig nor Hakonson would recognise him in his changed dress, provided he didn't speak too much. But it was better to play safe.

He didn't get a chance, however, to stay clear. Another voice joined in. This time it was Gruar. Alasdair saw his dark shape move forward and join the group.

"Good evening. I don't know any of you gentlemen, but my name is Gruar. I'm Mr. MacAra's new assistant."

Wynrame's voice, when he replied, was civil but bleak.

"Indeed, sir. I've been told about you. Are you alone?"

The doubt in the words was faint but unmistakable. Alasdair heard Gruar laugh.

"Fair enough. You're quite right to wonder. If you wait a few minutes, Macvartney the watcher will be here. I'm just waiting for him."

That settled it. Alasdair straightened up and walked towards the bridge, stepping deliberately on an outcrop of rock, making the nails in his shoe scrunch loudly.

Wynrame swung round and peered across the river.

"Who—oh, it's you, Macvartney."

There was no cordiality in the tone, but Alasdair was more concerned with Crossrig and Hakonson than with the keeper. If Naverack had been there things would have been more awkward, for Naverack had highly personal reasons for remembering him. Still, there was no option now. He took hold of the top wire and made his way along the bridge.

Across, he touched his cap to the group, then nodded to Wynrame.

"I'm taking Mr. Gruar down the river as far as Halmidary," he said, putting as much of a local accent as he dared into the words.

Wynrame turned to the two scientists.

"This is Macvartney, the river watcher. It's his job to look out for poachers too, but I didn't expect to find him so far up the river tonight. Are you expecting trouble, Macvartney?"

Alasdair was carefully casual.

"No, no. Just routine. Mr. Gruar wants to have a look around."

The American Hakonson laughed edgily.

"Looks as if you and I have just about gotten ourselves picked up as suspects, President. Do you reckon they want to search us?"

Even in the darkling his nervousness was obvious. Standing behind the little group, his face turned away from the scientists, Alasdair could still sense the tension at once. It took him longer to reassure himself that it couldn't have anything to do with Erica. Hakonson had sold that pass long ago. But the strain

was there for all that. In a better light he would have been able
to make out Hakonson's wide-set face, the creases at the corners
of his eyes, the iron-grey hair at his temples. Not that the sight
would have told him anything that he hadn't smelt already.
Leif Hakonson, confident Transatlantic technician, with his
London-cut suit and his hand-sewn shoes, was clamping down
hard on panic, and not doing it badly.

The scientist stamped his feet and rubbed his hands together.
Alasdair could see that his shoes were wet; indeed, he was
soaking up to the knees. He must be feeling the cold. Crossrig,
on the other hand, was dry-shod; he must have been handier at
crossing the bridge than his appearance suggested. The President was, however, beginning to get impatient. He looked
amiably but blankly at the other three men, giving no sign
whatever of having recognised Alasdair. Clearly, he wanted to
feed Hakonson with more physics. The American looked as if
he had had enough already, but the President's air of under-
standing and benevolence showed no signs of wilting.

"We'll say goodnight to you all then, unless you want to see
us safely off the river," he said. "But I can assure you that we
haven't been poaching—that is, if we could possibly poach when
we are staying here."

"Very good, sir," said Wynrame. "Good night. I'll just have
a word with Macvartney here before I go."

The two scientists walked off along the western bank towards
the farm, Crossrig talking hard as they went. Alasdair glanced
at his watch. The meeting had taken less than five minutes, but
it was almost half past eleven already.

Wynrame turned to Gruar.

"I beg your pardon, Mr. Gruar," he said.

"That's fair enough," Gruar replied. "No reason why you
should have believed me without proof."

He took out a packet of cigarettes. Alasdair took one, but
Wynrame shook his head. He laid his gun down whilst he
pulled a pipe from his pocket. Alasdair noticed that the weapon
was a Mannlicher stalking rifle—not quite what he would have
expected. If Wynrame was looking for foxes, as his wife had

said, a shot-gun would have made more sense; also, not even Wynrame would have dared to shoot at poachers with a high velocity rifle.

Wynrame lit a match, and held it to his pipe. The flare outlined his square chin, the deepset eyes above it, and a forelock of straw-coloured hair. There was a hint of impatience at the corners of his mouth.

"You'll be wanting to get on, I suppose." Wynrame said. It was a statement, not a question. "Which bank are you going down?"

"This one," Alasdair replied. "What about you?"

"I'm really after a fox that's been about these last few nights, so I'm going back across into the woods. Good night, Mr. Gruar. Good night, Macvartney."

He turned and splashed through the water on to the eastern bank. Gruar and Alasdair watched him go in silence.

"Not much of a conversationalist, is he?" Gruar said at last. "But come on. It's getting late. You lead the way, Alasdair."

*   *   *

A mile below the wire bridge the Blackwater swung sharply eastwards and disappeared into a gash in the hill face. Even against the wind a distant roaring came from the mouth of the gorge. It was the sound of the falls, a long series of rock slides down which the river tumbled, to emerge on the flats that could be seen from Halmidary. The path left the bank just above the narrows, and climbed straight over the low line of hills. The way was clear enough, even without a moon, for the dark of the Northern night was a relative thing only. Darkness, but in the open, was simply the absence of daylight; it had nothing of black about it.

At the top of the hill Alasdair stopped and pointed.

"That's the Devil's Pool there, just where the river comes into sight round that cliff," he said.

Gruar looked. The Devil's Pool was a pool to stand out anywhere, one of the finest stretches of fishing water north of the Spey. Forty yards long, deep on the eastern side where it undercut the hill, with a stream that never lost way even in the driest summer, it was small wonder that the Devil's Pool held fish, and those fish came to the fly, when everywhere else on the Blackwater was dour and dead. Alasdair had seen a dozen fish come out of it in a day, some of them upwards of twenty pounds in weight. It owed its name to a nineteenth-century minister—too interested in sport for the liking of a dour congregation—who slipped into it early one Monday morning and was drowned. The parish had long suspected him of putting his boots on before the Sabbath was out, and there was a good deal of quiet satisfaction that, so to speak, he had finally been hooked himself.

Tonight the Pool was running quietly. Alasdair pulled out his glasses and studied it carefully. The latent power of the current was obvious enough. From the race at the head to the long black rock at the foot, a line of foam eddied and swirled; beyond it little waves lapped at the edge of the bank. Alasdair shivered. The water was black and threatening.

He passed the glasses to Gruar. The assistant factor took his time. He looked at the Devil's Pool, then put the glasses over the long series of twisting flats that ran downstream as far as the railway bridge, two miles away. Finally he closed the glasses with a snap and handed them back to Alasdair.

"It's a good pool. I can see that," he said. "I'd like to fish it some day. Where do we go now, Alasdair?"

"We can go on as far as the bridge, if you like, Mr. Gruar, but there's no sign of anyone moving down there."

"Are you expecting to find poachers tonight?"

"No. One chance in a thousand, I should think, with this dance on."

Gruar seemed undecided. He stood up and looked at the sky. The clouds were thicker and lower. The rain was very close. If confirmation was needed, it came. The wind, previously steady from the south-west, dropped abruptly. The silence that followed was startling. Through it the sound of the falls rose sharply.

Gruar cocked a questioning eye at Alasdair.

"I don't like the wind dropping," Alasdair said. "The rain will be on us soon now."

"What I was thinking myself," said Gruar. "What's the quickest way back to Halmidary?"

"If you don't mind getting your feet wet, we'll be best to cut back to the river just above the falls and wade across. Then we can get on to the road from Craggan. It means a bit of a climb, but it'll save a mile in the long run."

"Come on, then," Gruar said.

They moved quickly now, through long heather, sloping across the hillside towards the river. The wind began to blow again, this time bringing a fine rain with it. Once off the hillside, Alasdair slackened pace. They reached the river bank, and dropped on to a narrow beach of coarse sand. Beyond, the river ran shallow over gravel shoals, with here and there a projecting rock. They scrunched across the gravel and into the water. Alasdair shivered as it flooded into his boots.

There was a boulder ahead, with an eddy of deep water at its foot. He turned slightly downstream to avoid it.

There was something odd about the eddy, he noticed. A dead sheep, perhaps.

But it wasn't a dead sheep, not even a dead stag. It was a dead man.

After a little while Gruar spoke.

"We'll have to get him out of there."

The man was lying face downward, half in and half out of the water. Alasdair got hold of his feet, Gruar gripped him under the armpits, and they lurched over to the further bank, splashing and stumbling. A heave, and the load was up on the grass. Another heave, and it was lying face upwards to the dark sky.

Gruar took a torch out of his pocket and flashed it on. Alasdair stood beside him, feeling sick. The rain became much heavier, hissing on the leaves of the birch trees.

"Who is he?" Gruar said.

"I don't know," Alasdair replied slowly. "I've never seen him in my life before."

CHAPTER THREE

"You'd be as well to start with the law of Scotland," said Inspector Cattanach.

Gruar had served his apprenticeship in an Edinburgh law-office, but he let the Inspector have his head. Cattanach was a red-faced, moustached man, who looked what he had been in his youth, an expert at tossing the caber and throwing the hammer at every Highland Games from Dornoch to Aboyne. He knew his county, and knew his job too. But whether he had imagination, and whether he was capable of rising to an emergency, were questions yet to be answered. For the moment MacAra's advice was sound—"take him slowly, and you'll maybe get somewhere; hurry him, and he'll go dour."

Cattanach took Gruar's silence as an invitation to continue. MacAra, walled in by stacks of deeds and papers, sat at his desk, watching. Varnished pine and the immense map of the county set him off perfectly. An anachronism, perhaps, but a worthwhile one. Gruar, leaning beside the tall window of the lawyer's office, looked at the old man with affection.

Outside the sky was clear again. The river was running high, but the rain of the night before had gone, leaving the soft brown stones of the Rhintraid breakwater washed clean. Few ships came to the harbour now. The river mouth was treacherous, and there was no longer coal to bring in or herring to take out. A few lobster fishermen had the quay to themselves, and MacAra's window looked on to the jibs of disused cranes and the carcasses of two rotting "Zulu" boats.

Cattanach cleared his throat.

"Well, then, the first point is that in Scotland the local court is the Sheriff's court, and the Sheriff is a real judge, not one of these ornamental things they have in England. In his court the

Crown is represented by a man we call the Procurator-Fiscal, who prosecutes in the Queen's name. It's his job to investigate any crime or apparent crime that happens in the county, and also any deaths arising from accident. So you'll see, Mr. Gruar, that the man you found has to be dealt with by the Procurator.

"What happens is roughly this. The police make enquiries and take statements and then pass them on to the Procurator. He has to send up a report to what we call the Crown Office in Edinburgh—the Crown's solicitors in Scotland. They pass the report on to Crown Counsel, and in the end the Procurator gets an instruction telling him what to do. Of course, it's often simple enough. In a clear criminal case, he can go ahead and take sworn statements—precognitions, we call them—from witnesses. Then, when he's got his instructions, he will get a warrant from the Sheriff for arrest, and have the suspected person in the Sheriff's room for judicial examination as quick as he likes. We don't have any of that magistrate's court preliminary nonsense, by the way.

"An accident, though, is rather different. Deaths from industrial accidents need a public enquiry. In an ordinary case, however, if the Procurator's report makes it clear that it was certainly an accident, then Edinburgh will probably order no action at all. But—and this is important—if there is the least doubt about it having really been an accident, then the Procurator has to be much more careful. The law of Scotland is quite precise here. The safest way to protect a murderer is to decide that the death was an accidental one, and take precognitions from all concerned to establish the facts. For, once precognitions have been taken, then the law debars a prosecution against anyone who has made one, as far as the case in question is concerned."

Gruar said: "So you're not sure it was an accident?"

"Just so." The Inspector paused, and took a pair of spectacles from his pocket. "Now, Mr. Gruar," he went on, "I'm going to tell you what we've found out so far, and then you'll see why I'm in a difficulty here."

He opened a folder lying on the desk in front of him and riffled through the papers in it.

"You found the man," he said, "just before midnight yesterday. The body was certainly dead, but there were no traces of stiffening."

Gruar nodded.

Cattanach picked out another paper.

"Dr. Gorm, called in by the police, examined the body at 5 a.m. this morning, and found rigor mortis well advanced. After a message from the Scottish Office in Edinburgh, an immediate post-mortem examination was ordered. It shows that the cause of death was drowning. There were a number of bruises about the head and face, which most probably happened before death."

"You've worked quickly," Gruar said.

"Not as quickly as I'd have liked. It was a nuisance not being able to get the doctor until 5 o'clock. He was handling an emergency appendix case all night. But when Edinburgh told us to get moving, and to keep you informed, then we did get started. There are some points about this conference at Craggan, by the——"

MacAra coughed.

"You'd better use the back room if you want to talk about that," he said. "The details are none of my business, and the less I know the better."

"You're quite right," Cattanach said. "It's not all that easy to remember we're dealing with what they call matters of state."

He shifted in his chair, grinning awkwardly. So far the omens were neutral, Gruar thought. The Inspector might be awkward to handle. No local policeman liked being given orders, whether they came from Edinburgh or London.

"Your law's all right, Inspector," MacAra said. "I take it the point is that you haven't been able to identify the man, but you're inclined to suspect that he may have been murdered?"

"Just so, just so, Mr. MacAra. These bruises are a bit of a problem. The man could have been knocked unconscious and

then held under water. The doctor won't go further than saying that he died sometime between noon on Saturday and
around 11 o'clock at night, so we've quite a bit of time to
cover. And there are two other points. First, the man's pockets
contained remarkably little. Six pound notes, some silver, a
small torch of a common make, and some scraps of electric
wire. No marks on the clothes at all. Second, nobody has identified him."

Gruar straightened up and took a pencil from his pocket.
Carefully he tapped at a somnolent bluebottle on the window
ledge. The fly toppled off, buzzed indignantly, and zigzagged
away across the room. Cattanach eyed it distrustfully. Gruar
grinned at him.

"Who have you asked to identify him?" he asked.

"Everyone at Craggan—and that includes the farm—has
been shown a large-scale photograph. Sergeant Ross is taking
one round Halmidary now. If he doesn't report in the next
half-hour, we can assume that he's had no luck."

"And besides that?"

"We were on to the railway offices at Inverness first thing
this morning. So far there's no report that anyone saw a man
aged about fifty, 5 ft. 6 in. tall, with black hair, on any train
north of Inverness yesterday. Also, they are satisfied that they
can account for all tickets issued yesterday. It wasn't a busy
day, and all the guards involved are quite sure about it."

"That doesn't rule out the railway, though," Gruar said.

"No. The man could have jumped off a goods train at the
sharp curve just above the bridge on the road from Halmidary
to Craggan, where I'm told there is a speed restriction of 15
m.p.h. So we're circulating a photograph. It's gone to all the
hydro-electric camps and to the Dounreay contractors too.
There's just a chance that the man was a labourer trying to go
south without paying, but it's a pretty slim one."

"What about the road?"

"We've been lucky there, thanks to this dance at Halmidary
last night. When the body was found we thought it might be a
drunk from the dance, and we did a quick check. The result

was negative. Nobody was missing, and in this part of the country it would be pretty difficult to hide a stranger at a dance. Also, there are always couples out in the dark at these dances. Nobody saw any strange car about, so we're as near certain as can be that none went up the Craggan road last night. And, of course, it would be difficult to avoid being spotted earlier in the day."

Gruar took out a note book.

"Yes. I'll confirm that. I've got a man on watch at the station as a porter, and he saw nothing but the Craggan farm truck, the shooting brake from the lodge, Constable Thomson's car, and myself and Macvartney the watcher. He was on duty until 11.30. I imagine you are ruling out any chance that the dead man went through later."

Cattanach made some notes in his file.

"Just so. We know about the cars that did go up the road. Thomson was meeting Wynrame the Craggan keeper to discuss poaching, and then ran him home. Mrs. Jardine from the farm was at the concert, and had Mrs. Wynrame with her. There were four people from the lodge in the brake. They had some drinks at the hotel, and went home before nine o'clock."

He paused to fill his pipe. Gruar looked out of the window. Down on the quayside a large red van was jolting its way across the cobbles towards the fishermen's cottages that lined the edge of the estuary. The sunlight showed up the letters on its side —"Winesack's Supermarkets".

Cattanach tossed the match into the fireplace behind him, and stuffed his papers into his file. He pushed his chair back and stretched out his legs.

"Look at it this way," he said. "The Procurator is going to be after me at the beginning of the week, and I'm anxious to have some sort of report to give him. I'd be a lot happier if I could identify the man. I'd also be happier if I knew a bit more about the situation at Craggan."

There was a short pause before MacAra spoke.

"What would you like to know?"

"Forgetting Wattie Jardine and his wife, and old Mrs.

Macrae the housekeeper, and her daughter the maid at Craggan,
there are seven people who interest me. Four guests at the
lodge—President Crossrig, Professor Naverack, Professor and
Mrs. Hakonson; Wynrame the keeper and his wife; and
Macvartney the river watcher. Can you help me at all? The
more I know about them, the sooner I can get moving."

"I know a bit about Wynrame," MacAra said. "By his own
story he is the son of an Orkneyman, born in Canada, who
learned his trade there as a game warden, and then came back
over as a sort of keeper-bodyguard to an American millionaire
who had an estate in Argyllshire. When the millionaire got
tired and sold up Wynrame stayed on in Scotland. The lawyers
in Oban who managed the American's place gave him a good
enough chit, and old Vaus thought that he might be a useful
sort of man to have about—would keep his mouth shut, and
wouldn't get involved too much with the locals. Vaus is a bit
touchy about Craggan—feels that people here think that he's
turned it into a sort of circus—and he doesn't mix much when
he comes up in the autumn. Wynrame suits him fine, and so
far they haven't fallen out, though Wynrame isn't much of a
hand at the keepering. I don't see much of him except for paying
him and sending tradesmen to do repairs at Craggan. I did
once try to check back with the American millionaire, but the
man seems to have disappeared somewhere east of Calcutta. All
I know about Mrs. Wynrame is that she isn't British born, and
though they apparently got married in the States I don't think
she is an American either. She's an interesting woman, and
an attractive one."

Cattanach grunted. Gruar watched the red van move along
the row of cottages, an escort of seagulls wheeling overhead.

"And the guests at the lodge?" said Cattanach.

Gruar turned to look at him.

"I can tell you a little about them. All the men are distinguished scholars. Professor Hakonson is an American,
Crossrig and Naverack both come from the University of Perth.
Mrs. Hakonson is the Professor's third wife; she's an American
too."

The Inspector was impressed. Gruar knew enough about his own race to realise that respect for learning was the Scots form of snobbery. MacAra, he saw out of the corner of his eye, was less at ease.

"That leaves Macvartney," Cattanach said. "Mind you, I'm not saying anyone at Craggan murdered the man. I'm not even saying he was murdered. I just want to get a picture of the people up there. If I have to ask questions and try to get them to help me, it's as well to know a bit about them."

He looked straight at MacAra as he finished speaking. It was the piece of evidence Gruar was looking for; the Inspector was on top of his job.

MacAra picked up a paper-weight from the desk and played with it before replying. When he spoke he looked older.

"You'd be a fool if you didn't keep an open mind," he said. "Macvartney—that's not his real name, incidentally—answered an advertisement I put in the papers for a watcher. He hadn't any qualifications for the job, but he sounded interesting, so I went to Inverness and saw him. Then I got some information from a couple of old friends, and as a result I took him on. He's done his work well, and I trust him."

"I'm sure you're right to do so," said the Inspector. "But can you tell me any more about him? After all, he's a stranger in the strath, and I've known most of the people there since I was a boy."

"Yes." MacAra's voice was suddenly decisive. "I'll tell you more. But first I'll say one thing. Macvartney has been badly hurt not so very long ago. He had to resign from his own profession. Possibly he was stupid; he certainly wasn't a criminal. But the resignation was final. He can't go back. All he wants to do is to be accepted here and go to ground in the strath. You must be careful with him, for I find him pretty useful. That's my price for telling you any more."

"Just so, just so. I hope you'll trust me, Mr. MacAra."

MacAra smiled.

"I'm sure I can, Inspector. I knew you when you were a new constable, and I've always trusted you. So you can know that

D

Macvartney used to be a lecturer at the University of Perth. I don't know the details, but Professor Naverack had something to do with his resignation."

Gruar turned back to the window. In the silence that followed the bluebottle banged against the window and slithered down the glass on to the ledge. The red van was back on the quay again. As Gruar watched, it slowed down to turn up between two roofless warehouses towards the main road. Then it stopped. A figure in blue uniform walked down the road. The driver clambered down and went to the rear door of the van. He opened it, and both men got in. Gruar had seen the man in blue earlier in the morning. It was Constable Thomson.

Behind him Cattanach got to his feet without looking at MacAra.

"Thank you, Mr. MacAra," he said. "I'll use that information carefully. Now perhaps I ought to go to the back room with Mr. Gruar and talk business. One last thing. How tall are the men at the lodge?"

"The President is 6 ft. 3 in. Quite unmistakable. As for Naverack, he's a very short man. I doubt if he's much over 5 ft. So——"

MacAra broke off. It was some time before he continued. When he did he spoke very quietly.

"So I don't think you can suggest that it would be possible to mistake the dead man for either of them. The only person at Craggan who might fit for height is Hakonson, and he's not from Perth."

He turned on his heel and stared at the map behind him. He didn't move when Gruar walked softly out behind Cattanach and closed the door.

*   *   *

Gruar shut the door of the back room and turned the key.

"I've tested this room for microphones," he said. "We can talk here."

"You're suspicious," said Cattanach. "Are you expecting Mr.

MacAra to listen in? I'll vouch for him myself, if you like. He's helped me often enough before."

Gruar shrugged.

"Call it professional habit. But it doesn't pay to take chances in this game. Now, Inspector, can you give me a report?"

"Yes. Your department will get all the co-operation you asked for. The telephone people are fixing a scrambler in our office at Dalbreck this morning, so you can get in touch from Craggan from lunch-time on. I've detailed a plain clothes man to go with that radio car you sent us. I could do with one of these for myself—I've asked for one often enough, but this county never seems to have the money to spare. The Caithness and Sutherland police have been alerted too. I'd have liked to stop all leave here for next week, but you were probably right to advise against it; no point in making too much noise unless we have to. What about your end?"

Gruar grinned.

"If anything, too well covered from today on. I've had one man at the station all week, and tonight a dozen foresters will be squatting in the stables at Craggan, ready to start work in the woods on Monday. There are three rather senior men staying in the lodge, taking turns at fishing the river. I hope they remember to do more than fish; it's remarkable how much competition there was for that part of the assignment. And of course, four of the extra house staff who are coming up from London on the afternoon train are our men. My chief worry is that they're all going to fall over each other."

"Just so," Cattanach was impressed. "What about the timing of the whole business?"

"No change from what I told you last week. It's just a damned nuisance that Crossrig arranged with Vaus to bring his friends up early for a holiday, and didn't think to tell us. The main party of delegates arrives tomorrow evening, and the conference begins on Monday morning. It's scheduled to end on Wednesday, not later than 6 o'clock, and they all go off by coach to catch the evening plane at Wick. From midnight tonight we'll have patrols out. Anyone going near Craggan will need a pass signed either by you, MacAra, or myself. That lasts until midnight on Wednesday."

"I see. It seems a terrible elaborate business." Catternach's accent was broadening. "We never had this nonsense with any of the other conferences at Craggan."

"Agreed. But then we're having to make rather extra preparations ourselves. I never liked the idea of this conference being at Craggan. It's far easier to rig up real security in a city than here, where everything we do sticks out a mile. My masters don't like it either. However, we've got to do what we're told. This is a small conference, but top-secret and international. That's why I'm here, and why I've been spending so much time wandering around Halmidary and Craggan these last two days. Are the details quite clear?"

Cattanach nodded. He tapped restlessly on the edge of the table with his pencil, then looked straight at Gruar.

"Where do you think this drowned man fits in?" he asked.

"I'd like very much to know," Gruar replied. "And I'd like to know some other things also."

"Such as?"

"How and when he got to Craggan. Why Crossrig and Hakonson were out so late last night. Why Wynrame was carrying a deer rifle, yet said he was out hunting foxes. Why the poachers keep coming back to the strath."

"I suppose you've got to be suspicious all the time," said Cattanach. "But I'd have thought some of these might be my business as much as yours. Take Macvartney. Did you see him yourself at the hotel?"

"Yes. It would be interesting to know more about his leaving Perth. However, MacAra believes in him."

"Aye. And that's a point, I can tell you, Mr. Gruar. Mr. MacAra's not very often wrong about people. You'd wonder why, sometimes; he used to be a wild enough character himself. But I trust him. All the same, if it had been one of the people from Perth who was dead I'd be doing a bit of wondering myself. But I don't see where the poachers come in."

"Neither do I. It's just that there's something unusual about it, and the unusual interests me this week. Will you do something for me, Inspector?"

"Surely. What is it?"

"If I get someone to keep an eye on McGlashan, and tip me off if he comes north, will you have your men ready to watch him?"

"Yes. We'll try. I hope there's not something more important happening at Craggan."

"Good."

Gruar got to his feet and walked across to the door. He put his hand on the key, then turned to Cattanach.

"How long can you hold the Procurator-Fiscal off?" he asked.

"Till Monday, certainly. Perhaps a couple of days longer. If I don't get the man identified we may be able to avoid making formal enquiries for several days—except for trying to establish identity, that is. But that can't last indefinitely, and anyway I've got to go on trying."

"I see," Gruar said. "A few days would be a help. I'll set some wheels turning myself."

"Where are you going now?" Cattanach asked, as Gruar turned the key.

"I'm taking Macvartney up to Corrachan. He's standing in for the keeper there. And I'm going to call at Craggan lodge on the way. There are some small repairs MacAra wants me to look at. Wynrame can show me the way round."

He pulled the door shut, and re-locked it carefully. Cattanach went out into the hall and through the frosted-glass swing doors. Gruar gave him five minutes to get clear, then followed.

He walked across to his car, got in, and lit a cigarette. He was just moving off on the Halmidary road when the red van he had seen on the quayside passed, going south. The driver, he noticed, was alone.

CHAPTER FOUR

"T H I S didn't get on the road by accident," Gruar said, tapping the stone with his foot. "Why MacCrossich's ditch, anyway?"

"MacCrossich used to be the doctor in Rhintraid," Alasdair replied. "I gather he was liable to put his car into this ditch after an evening with the old laird. It got to be such a habit that the coachman always had a pair of horses waiting to pull the car out. But that's a big stone."

Gruar made no comment. They were less than a couple of hundred yards from Craggan lodge. Behind them Gruar's car stood at the fork in the road that led to Corrachan. It was early afternoon, and the sun was high in the sky. The rhododendron bushes glistened, washed clean by the overnight rain. Alasdair watched an early horse-fly circle purposefully round the leaves. Away on the moor behind the trees came the comfortable Victorian sound of a cock-grouse, warning the other members of his club that he spied strangers. The river was full, the salmon were running up over the falls, and he was on his way to Corrachan.

"A car would have to be coming pretty fast to get into real trouble with the stone," Gruar said after a pause. "But a driver seeing it would be very likely to swerve, and then he would end up in the ditch. Was that the point?"

He turned and looked straight at Alasdair.

"What do you mean?" Alasdair said uncomfortably.

"That stone wasn't on the road when I walked past at about half past nine last night. But it was there about an hour later. It could have been put there to stop cars coming past here. Did you see it as you came to the farm?"

Alasdair shook his head.

"I didn't come this way. I went down the path past the

54

kennels"—he pointed at the high fence showing over the rhododendrons—"so the stone could perfectly well have been on the road without my knowing anything about it. But why should anyone have put it there?"

Gruar shrugged.

"Inspector Cattanach is a policeman. What do you think he would say about that?"

Alasdair was silent a moment before accepting the gambit. Gruar wanted him to talk. All at once it was easier to do that than to try to keep up the barrier.

"I'd think," he said slowly, "that the Inspector would wonder if there was any connection between the stone and the dead man we found in the river."

"And so——"

"And so he would think about the various people who were about here last night. Is that what you want me to say?"

The horse-fly dropped neatly on to Gruar's wrist. Gruar smacked at it with his other hand, missed, and swore softly as he sucked at the white circle of the bite. The fly swept away towards the house. Gruar puffed at his cigarette.

"You've taken the point, I see, Alasdair. So you won't be surprised to know that Cattanach is interested in your past?"

"No. Not very surprised. And what has he found out about it?"

The antagonism in his voice made Gruar look up quickly.

"As much as you would expect. He knows that you used to be at Perth University, and that Professor Naverack was involved in your dismissal. It may be just as well for you that the dead man was nothing at all like Naverack."

"Are you a policeman yourself?" Alasdair asked.

Gruar laughed.

"No. I'm not a policeman, and I won't go telling Inspector Cattanach anything you say to me."

"So what's your interest in all of this?"

Gruar threw his cigarette down and stood on it. The horse-fly reappeared above a rhododendron bush.

"Let's say simply that I'm interested in people—particularly people I like. Would you like to tell me just why you came to work here?"

"Because I hadn't very much choice. I wasn't prepared to teach in a school, and I didn't want to become a bit of cultural driftwood in London or anywhere else. Mr. MacAra's advertisement seemed a way out, so I applied for the job. He took me on, though I didn't find out until later that he had contacts at Perth."

Gruar nodded. He took out his wallet, opened it, and handed Alasdair a folded paper.

"Keep that," he said. "As from tonight until Wednesday evening you won't be allowed through the lodge grounds here without showing it."

"Another conference?" Alasdair asked.

"Yes. I suppose that isn't a surprise to you?"

"Not exactly. They happen fairly often. But——"

He let the sentence die on the air.

"But what?" Gruar asked.

Alasdair was silent for a few seconds.

"Nothing. I'm not inquisitive. But there is one thing you can tell Inspector Cattanach, if you like."

"And that is—?"

"Just that the American Hakonson was a visiting professor at Perth for a year. He'll have noticed that the dead man is very much Hakonson's build."

Gruar ignored the bitterness in Alasdair's tone. He lit another cigarette and passed the packet to Alasdair.

"Tell him yourself, if he asks you. Now, come on. I've got to go over the lodge and check some repair jobs that the joiner was doing last week. We'll start by finding Wynrame."

* * *

Wynrame was feeding retrievers in the kennels. He straightened up as Gruar and Alasdair approached. The dogs behind him began to bark.

"Good afternoon, Mr. Gruar," Wynrame said, above the random chorus.

"Good afternoon, Wynrame." Gruar was formal. "Has the joiner finished in the lodge?"

"He finished on Thursday, Mr. Gruar," Wynrame replied. "Are you wanting to see what he did? I think the guests in the lodge are all out just now."

"Good enough. We'll just go and have a tour of inspection."

"Very good, Mr. Gruar. I'll put my jacket on."

Wynrame pulled the kennel door shut. The click of the lock was echoed by a sharp crack from the direction of the lodge. Gruar, who was bending down to tie a shoelace, looked up quickly.

Wynrame answered his unspoken question.

"It looks as if one of the guests hasn't gone out. That'll be Professor Naverack practising at the target with the stalking rifle. He has it out most evenings."

"I see," Gruar said. "Perhaps I ought to meet him before we go to the lodge. A matter of politeness, after all. What sort of a rifle is he using?"

"A Mannlicher—there's only the one stalking rifle in the gun-room."

"What do you use yourself?"

"I haven't got a rifle," Wynrame said over his shoulder, leading the procession through the shrubbery. "I take the lodge one when I need it."

Along the front of the lodge fuchsias ran riot, half-heartedly restrained by a low wooden fence. Beyond the gravel sweep of the drive a row of trees fringed a long lawn, blotchy with light-green moss. But it was the trees that dominated. Alasdair had seen many monkey-puzzles since he had come to the Highlands. They were a Victorian affectation that had got out of hand, and now they darkened the doorways of hotels, concealed the corrugated-iron beauties of village halls. He had even seen a whole grove of them, planted long ago in a ducal forest nursery. They were out of place, but at least they didn't apologise for it, like the pathetic travesties of palms in hotel gardens along the extreme north coast. Monkey-puzzles had no modesty; one of those in front of him came within half a dozen feet of a window on the upper floor of the lodge; the effect from inside must be overpowering.

At the far end of the lawn stood a large painted stag, a bright circle of white marking the vital target area around its heart. As they watched there was another sharp crack, and the stag shook briefly. Alasdair looked round. Under one of the monkey puzzles a man was lying with a rifle. Even from the unfamiliar angle it was impossible to mistake Naverack; the cock-sparrow sharpness, the unquestioning confidence communicated themselves at once. What couldn't be seen, Alasdair thought, was the soft line of the mouth, the faint but uncontrollable exaggeration of gesture, the shadowy second personality behind the professorial façade. But nobody, even in the half-dark, could ever have confused the Professor of Entrepreneurial Ethics with the dead man in the river.

He stood back, letting Gruar and Wynrame advance on Naverack. The Professor would certainly recognise him at close quarters, and there was no need for that.

The rifle cracked, and the painted stag shuddered. But it didn't make sense. Naverack with a rifle was an improbability, as unlikely as the southerners in tweeds who would be crowding the strath in August. Besides, there wasn't anything to use a stalking rifle on in June. And yet, Alasdair realised as he stood in the shelter of the fuchsias, perhaps it did make a certain kind of sense. Power and play-acting were Naverack's stock in trade: he had played the administration man, he had played the academic man, now he was playing the sporting gentleman. It was his fatality that the disguises never quite fitted. The false nose was always too big, the painted moustache always too implausible. A touch of humanity, and the man might have been a great comedian. As it was, Alasdair saw in a second of clarity, he was simply a corrupted corrupter; it was beside the mark to think of him as a man of power. Hating Naverack, blaming Naverack for what had happened at Perth—all at once these ceased to be necessary, became no longer relevant.

Wynrame stopped suddenly and felt his pockets.

"I'll need to get my keys, Mr. Gruar," he said. "I must have left them at the house. It won't take me five minutes."

"Macvartney can go, if you like," Gruar said quickly. "I'd like you to give me a few tips on handling that rifle. Can your wife find the keys for him?"

Wynrame's pause was perceptible, as calculating as Gruar's speed. Then the keeper nodded.

"Surely. Tell my wife, Macvartney, to look in the kitchen dresser."

Naverack had just realised that there were people watching him. He began to climb stiffly to his feet. Alasdair turned and walked away.

Ann Wynrame came to the door when he knocked. She was wearing slacks, and her black hair was hanging loose. Alasdair avoided her eyes as he explained what he wanted, trying not to see the smile that flickered across her mouth.

"Of course. Just wait a minute, Alasdair."

She went into the kitchen. Through the open door Alasdair could see the cool, dark hall, and beyond it the white walls of the kitchen. Behind him a wood-pigeon was crying softly in the trees. He felt himself sliding helplessly down a long slope.

Ann came back, the keys in her hand. She had tied her hair loosely back, and her eyes were smiling now.

"Here you are."

She held out the keys. Alasdair took hold of them, then let his hand stay where it was. For the first time he looked straight at her. He felt her fingers close over his own. The slope steepened, and he hurtled downwards.

He took a deep breath and moved closer to her. With her other hand she held him away.

"No. Not now. You must take these keys to the lodge."

He relaxed and stepped back. Her grip slackened, and with a jolt he reached the bottom of the slope.

"Tell Mr. Gruar I'll have tea ready for you both when he's finished," Ann said in a flat voice.

"I want to see you—soon," said Alasdair.

"Wait. There's plenty of time. You must go now."

Gruar and Wynrame were standing in the gun-room, on the left of the front door, when he found them. Gruar had the Mannlicher in his hands. He pulled back the bolt, tested the magazine, released the trigger, and then squinted along the telescopic sight. Wynrame watched him.

"Very handy," said Gruar, balancing the compact, vicious weapon in one hand. "Do you like it, Wynrame?"

"It's very good, Mr. Gruar. I hope Professor Naverack wasn't too annoyed that I took it last night. I never thought he would be wanting it, and when I found it on the hall table I just picked it up without asking."

"I wouldn't worry," said Gruar. "He seemed quite happy when he went off for his walk just now."

He ran his hand along the glass case that filled one wall. Taking out an enormous gun, he looked at it curiously.

"That's an elephant gun," Wynrame explained. "I've never seen it used, and I don't know if it's safe to fire now. It's pretty old."

No elephants in the strath today. Seven hundred years ago there had been reindeer, two hundred years ago wolves. Now there were only red deer and grey foxes—and somewhere a rogue human, with no flapping ears or gleaming tusks to mark him out. Elephants would have been less disconcerting.

Gruar finished looking at the guns. Wynrame shut the case and locked it. Alasdair handed over the bunch of keys Ann Wynrame had given him.

At the first door at the head of the stairs Wynrame paused and juggled with the keys. He selected one and opened the door. It showed a large room—a cross between a drawing-room and a conference chamber, with armchairs and a large central table.

"This used to be the library in the old days," the keeper said. "But Sir John keeps all his books in London now, and the book-cases are boxed up."

Nothing more morbid than a library stripped of its books. Vaus had been sensible, even if the result had been to give the walls a curiously streaky appearance, for the wood used to cover up the shelves was younger than the plain fir wainscoting and was weathering only slowly. Now the room looked arid but businesslike, a superior setting for adult education classes and summer schools.

Gruar walked from window to window, testing the long cords, opening and shutting each in turn. Wynrame went in front of him, releasing the catches which secured the windows from the unlikely attentions of burglars. Alasdair stood back, and looked idly round the room. The boxing-in of the shelves had not been very carefully done, he noticed. One or two of the wood panels were warping, and one at least gaped at a corner.

Gruar, his job finished, dusted his hands and came across to join Alasdair while Wynrame refastened the windows. That done, they all turned to go. As they did so Gruar caught his foot against the edge of a chair, and stumbled. The notebook and pencil which he held fell to the floor. He swore briefly, bent down and groped for them. The pencil had rolled under a chair. Eventually Alasdair took hold of the chair and tilted it out of the way. Gruar got up, holding the pencil, and straightened his jacket.

"Clumsy," he said. "I'm always doing that."

They left the conference room, and went into a series of bed-rooms along the corridor that ran the length of the floor. In each room Gruar tested the window, though less carefully than in the library. Alasdair looked at the rooms curiously. Craggan might be Victorian in origin, but Vaus had brought it up to date. No marble slabs and rococo ewers, but running water in each room, a series of modern prints, and a carefully selected shelf of superior books. The present occupants had left some traces of themselves. A battered Gladstone bag in one room must belong to Crossrig, who affected such things. Two bulky American books on business management and a sheaf of company reports signalled Naverack's room. In the last room of all, two shiny airline suitcases and a pile of glossy travel books showed the tracks of the Hakonsons. As Gruar looked at the windows, Alasdair picked the books up and flicked idly through their pages. Italy, France, the Dalmatian coast, southern Germany, Copenhagen—the intelligent American's guide to European fossils. The last book of all caught his eye: mountain landscapes in Norway, superbly photographed. A bookmark fluttered out as he turned the pages, and fell to the floor. Wynrame picked it up, glanced at it, and handed it back to Alasdair. It was a postcard. Casually Alasdair turned it over. It showed mountain slopes taken from a dizzy height, with houses and fields stretched along the valley bottom.

Gruar had finished his inspection of the windows. He leaned out of one of them and gazed westwards across the valley to the hill beyond. Alasdair put the book down. Over Gruar's shoulder he could see Wattie moving up the side of the hill towards the skyline, his dogs half-hidden in the heather in front of him.

"The best bedroom in the house, I should think," said Gruar. "That's a beautiful view, though it's a pity that someone planted that monkey-puzzle tree so close."

"The tree's got too big, I'm afraid, sir," said Wynrame, "but Sir John isn't keen to have it cut down, and so it stays. It's only at one corner that it really spoils the view."

Gruar brought his head in again and closed the window.

"What's left to look at?" he asked Wynrame. "The joiner seems to have fixed these window cords."

"There are two cupboard doors in the scullery," said Wynrame. "And I'd like you to have a look at one of the kitchen sinks. There's a big crack in it, and I think it would be as well to replace it."

"Right. That won't take us long. Alasdair, you could go across and tell Mrs Wynrame I'll be finished in ten minutes, and then I'll be very glad to take up her offer of a cup of tea."

Again the calculation. Alasdair saw Wynrame's eyes flicker from his own face to Gruar's, and then back again. He kept his face steady, nodded, and went off down the stairs. For an instant he was angry at Gruar; the man was making him a marionette. But the anger didn't last. It was more important that he was going to be alone with Ann.

*   *   *

The sitting-room was a surprise. No Landseers, no coloured calendars, no ornamental cupboard full of Victorian china. But books, lots of books—German, French, and, he thought, Norwegian. Two violent Utrillo prints, full of Southern heat and sun, and over against them a striking photograph. At first sight he thought of Glencoe, then looked more closely. He had seen a photograph of the same valley not half an hour before—in the Hakonsons' bedroom. Norway, perhaps, or Switzerland—it ought to be identifiable. The room, too, was a problem in identification, for it struck a note of personality, a hint at the contradictions in the keeper and his wife. North and South: the olive trees and the blue sea, the upland meadows and the snow-crested peaks. A salmon rod and a shotgun, stacked in a corner, seemed half-hearted attempts at camouflage, a native fancy-dress that only drew attention to the foreigner underneath. It was a room with its guard half-down.

He roamed restlessly about, picking up first one book and then another, trying to avoid thinking. He was flicking through a volume of German poems when the door opened and Ann came in with a tray. He put the book down hurriedly and took the tray from her, to set it on a table. She shut the door and looked at him with amusement.

"Not what one of the real natives would do, you know. This isn't a country where men help in the house. You'll have to do better than that if you're going to stay here. There's a conference starting tomorrow, and the security men will be taking a good look at you."

Alasdair placed the tray carefully on the table.

"That man we found in the river last night—do you think he was murdered?" he asked.

The effect was unexpected. For an instant she was remote and impersonal, like an adder coiled black and diamond beside a stone. He thought of the ruined brochs down the strath, their stones as grey and secretive as her face. But he wasn't repelled; things were getting beyond that.

Then she shrugged, and smiled.

"Leave that to the police. If they think he was, they will be asking questions soon enough."

She put her hand on his shoulder and pulled him round and away from the window. Her other hand slipped round his back and she put up her face to his. The first kiss was neither long nor enjoyable. He was being trapped into a ludicrous error in a game of forfeits. He kissed her again, and this time it was different.

After a time she pushed him away, and stepped back to look at him. She smiled, and the bond of complicity was complete. So much for the ivory tower, he thought.

"It took you a long time," she said, smiling at some secret pleasure of her own. "Now you'd better wipe that lipstick off your face and have a cup of tea."

Alasdair took out his handkerchief and scrubbed at his face. He balanced himself on the edge of a chair and took the cup that she offered.

"A long time," he repeated. "Cold feet. I've had them about you for a long time. I remember thinking last night that my feet were probably colder than Professor Hakonson's, even though he was soaked up to the knees. Now——"

"Hakonson fell into the river, didn't he?" Ann asked.

"Falling is my business right now. He certainly didn't tumble off the bridge when he crossed it. I'm sure of that. Your husband could tell you, for he was there too. I'm positive Hakonson's feet were wet already. But I think I took longer to warm up than he did."

She smiled and relaxed in her chair, watching him contentedly. Now her mood had changed again.

"Has anybody identified the dead man?" she asked.

"Mr. Gruar says no—at least, not by noon today. Do you think he was the man we saw when we were walking back from the farm?"

She shook her head.

"I don't know. Do the police know about that, by the way?"

"I haven't told them yet, and I'm not hurrying to."

"Why?"

"I want to keep myself to myself," Alasdair said. "They can get on with their own work."

"If they ask you questions will you tell them about it?"

Alasdair didn't answer at once.

"I suppose I would," he said at last. "Hiding things is liable to be awkward. But——"

He broke off. What he wanted to say was that there was a woman at the lodge whom he had slept with, that he never wanted to see her again; he wanted to explain everything that ever happened to him. It didn't matter that a few minutes before he had seen in Ann's face the look of a hunting animal. There was a lot to tell her, wherever she might fit in to the hidden pattern that was swirling around him.

But telling was difficult. The shield he had built round his hurt was too strong. He paused, and the moment was lost. There was the sound of feet outside. Then Gruar and Wynrame came in.

*   *   *

The car was in sight ahead. Gruar turned and looked back along the road. Wynrame was walking towards the lodge. He disappeared from sight round a bend, and Gruar looked satisfied.

"Can you drive, Alasdair?" he said.

"Yes, Mr. Gruar."

"Good. Now listen. Get into the car and drive up the Cor-rachan road as far as the first gate. That's about half a mile. Take your time about it. Once through the gate pull the car off the road. There's a passing place I spotted earlier this morning when I was up seeing Donald off in the ambulance. Wait there. I won't be long. Got that?"

E

"Yes." No point in asking questions; there would probably be no answers, anyway.

"Right. One thing more. Take these and hang on to them till I get back."

He passed over a handful of pieces of wire and metal, and slipped into the trees. Alasdair wrapped the pieces in his handkerchief, and walked on to the car.

The Corrachan track was rough. Clumps of rushes in the middle of the road swished continuously against the underside of the car. He drove slowly, thinking hard. Beyond the gate he found the passing place, and stopped.

It was half an hour before Gruar reappeared. He opened the car door and slid in.

"Drive on. Next stop Corrachan," he said.

There was silence for a long time. Gruar lit a cigarette and settled back in his seat.

"What do you think I've been doing, Alasdair?"

Again the invitation to talk. This time Alasdair found himself answering at once. The ivory tower was receding.

"Having a look at the lodge," he answered.

"And what did I see?"

"I imagine you saw Wynrame doing something at those windows you were so interested in."

"Almost. What I did see was Wynrame taking a ladder and climbing into that disgusting monkey-puzzle tree. I wonder why?"

"You may not be a policeman, Mr. Gruar, but you're behaving very like one."

Gruar laughed.

"Fair enough. Now where are these things I gave you?"

Alasdair took his left hand off the wheel and passed over the handkerchief. Gruar unwrapped it carefully.

"Three slivers of plastic-covered wire and two insulating staples. Not a usual British type, either."

"So what?" said Alasdair.

Gruar passed the handkerchief back.

"So nothing very much—yet. Incidentally, Inspector Cattanach doesn't know what we've been up to this afternoon. Nor"—he looked hard at Alasdair—"am I going to tell him that your handkerchief is heavily marked with what I can only take to be lipstick. He might get the wrong idea."

Alasdair, hauling the car round a hairpin bend, said nothing.

CHAPTER FIVE

B Y ten o'clock on Sunday morning it was clear that Donald's cow had won. Alasdair hunted through the dilapidated boat-house until he found a length of rope. Then he locked the gun-room, moist with the smell of oil, shut the lodge door, banked up the peat fire in the keeper's house, and set off to walk to Wattie's farm. One lesson from Wattie hadn't been enough. The cow needed milking, and he couldn't milk it; he had two bruises on his shoulder to show what the cow thought of his efforts. So there were four hot miles ahead of him.

At the head of the first rise he stopped and looked back at Corrachan. This was a different world from Craggan. No trees, no garden, only a cluster of corrugated-iron out-buildings, the keeper's cottage, the boat-house, and the little box of the lodge itself. Beyond, the Blackwater flowed out of Loch Skiag in a shallow, stony bed. To the east a sweep of low heather hills ran away to the skyline. And straight in front, across a mile of white-dappled water, rose Creag an Lochain—two thousand foot and more of rock and scree climbing sheer out of the loch to an unbelievably jagged ridge, with no heather and hardly any grass to break the greyness of its raw bones. Only at the far western end of the loch was there any change in the colour. There a streak of gold showed where the east wind had win-nowed down the rocks to sand. And to east, to west, and back to the south-west marched, with the precision of Roman roads, the bridle paths of the deer forest, gouges in the sea of heather, anchor lines for the solitary lodge.

The cow tugged at the improvised halter. Alasdair turned and set his feet to the twisting road. Two miles to the top of the ridge, another two down the far slope and into the Craggan woods. There were men in Halmidary who shaved late on Saturday night, to avoid breaking the sabbath; there were women whose Sunday cooking never went beyond making tea. But milking a cow was a permitted task, and here he was trudging the road, taking a cow to be milked, with the June sun blazing down. He was nearer to being a part of the strath than he had ever been. He began to whistle, tunelessly.

A mile from Craggan the road twisted over a narrow bridge and entered the wood. He was just approaching the bridge when a respectable-looking person in tweeds, a walking-stick in one hand and a gaff in the other, came out of the trees. The respectable-looking person was polite, but firm. Would Alasdair please identify himself? Alasdair did so, and thought better of enquiring just why his questioner was carrying a gaff during the sacred hours between six o'clock on Saturday night and six o'clock on Monday morning, when the law of Scotland extends sabbath observance to the benefit of the salmon and the sea-trout.

By the time he reached the farm Alasdair had shown his pass thrice, the last time to an individual with a brand new shepherd's crook, standing uncomfortably on the farm bridge. Alasdair resisted the temptation to talk sheep to him. It was becoming routine to be challenged. But his first sight of Wattie Jardine startled him.

Wattie was clearly having no ordinary Sunday. An expedition into the outer world was being planned, for standing in the farmyard was Wattie's elderly, angular car, a vehicle that rarely saw the light of day. Wattie was happier driving his truck. He had once even gone in it to the Highland Show at Aberdeen, Mrs. Jardine jolting beside him and a collie-dog complaining in the back.

Wattie received the cow without surprise or enthusiasm.

"Put her in the byre, Alasdair," he said, taking his pipe out of his mouth. "I'll get her milked now. You'll be leaving her here, I suppose?"

"If you'll take her," Alasdair replied cautiously.

"Of course. Another one won't worry us. But away you go

in and talk to the wife. I'll have to hurry, before this state occasion."

"And on the sabbath, I see," said Alasdair. "What's taking you out today?"

"The wife," Wattie said shortly. "You'd best go into the kitchen and find out for yourself. And mind you don't agree to anything she suggests."

Alasdair knocked and went in. Mrs. Jardine, under a formidable hat, was banking up the fire.

"It's yourself, Alasdair, is it?" she said. "You're just in time. You're not on business, I hope?"

"Not really," Alasdair admitted cautiously. "I've brought the cow down, and now I'm off to my cottage to get a book. But Wattie says I'm not to agree to anything you say."

"Does he, though?" Mrs. Jardine was indignant. "One of these days I'll give him a real surprise. But you've got time to come along with us, I hope. Unless you're meaning to go to the evening service, that is."

She knew well enough that Alasdair never went to the morning service, let alone the evening one. If there was anyone in the strath he disliked more than Wynrame, it was the Reverend Aeneas Mactorquil, minister of the united parishes of Rhintraid and Aultnachie. The dislike was mutual. The Reverend Aeneas, precise in the rigour of his Sunday theology, was a public figure of some consequence—County Councillor, Justice of the Peace, member of half a dozen boards and consultative committees, self-appointed protector of what he called "the pure beauty of Gaelic culture". MacAra had hated and fought him for years, and Alasdair—glad enough to rationalise the laziness which kept him from cycling to Rhintraid to hear a forty-minute sermon—had been quick to take the lawyer's side. So Mrs. Jardine was on safe enough ground.

"Where are you going?" he asked, hedging without any great hope of success. "I ought really to get back to Corrachan."

"Abroad, you might say. There's some sort of a regatta—whatever that might be—up at Invermudale, and I was thinking we might take a run up there."

This was unlikely, out of character, for yachting was not one of Mrs. Jardine's habitual interests. Alasdair tried to guess the inwardness of the idea, and failed. He looked at her. She was chuckling.

"You'll not work it out, Alasdair," she said, "seeing you weren't in church this morning."

"Ah, so that's it." Alasdair began to laugh too. "Has the Reverend Aeneas been denouncing this latest desecration of the sabbath, and are all his congregation going to have a look for themselves as a result?"

"Just that. You couldn't stop Wattie if you tried. Besides, there was talk after church that the minister himself was going to make a public protest at the end of Invermudale pier. You'll come with us? Mrs. Wynrame is coming too."

Alasdair started to excuse himself, thought better of it, and finally nodded his agreement. It wouldn't do to protest too much.

"I'll come," he said.

"Good. I'll just shut up the window and we can get off when Wattie's milked your cow—that is, if he's remembered to put any petrol in the car."

Wattie, it appeared, had been provident. He was sitting at the wheel, the car dancing in a cloud of blue smoke. Alasdair began to wonder if they would make the twenty miles north to Invermudale without catastrophe, for the machine seemed as apprehensive as the collie cowering at the byre-door.

Wattie waved to them to climb in. Alasdair moved to open the rear door for Mrs. Jardine, but she went past him and settled herself in the front beside her husband.

"You sit in the back with Mrs. Wynrame, Alasdair," she said. "I always like to have my hand near the brake when Wattie is driving."

Wattie, overdressed in a thick black suit, snorted. But Alasdair could see his face in the driving mirror, and it was a grinning face. Damn the two of them, he thought; they suspect what's happening and they aren't making it any easier for me.

"Doesn't Wynrame want to come?" he asked hopefully as

Wattie pointed the car at the bridge and the quailing pseudo-shepherd standing beside it.

"He can't," Mrs. Jardine replied. "He went off out on the hill early this morning. I don't know that he would be all that keen for his wife to come with us, but I told her that it was her duty as a member of the women's guild to support the minister."

The Reverend Aeneas, Alasdair reflected, would not feel much the better for the support. The minister's view of the guild was a simple one; he tolerated its existence because it kept the women of the strath away from the men and from more dangerous activities than the gatherings over which he himself presided. The guild, aware of his estimate of them, retaliated by conducting their meetings with a maximum of gossip and ferocity, in nicely judged proportions. By and large the women won on points. But none of that made Mrs. Jardine's story any more plausible, Alasdair felt uneasily. He was as little in control of the situation as the Reverend Aeneas was of his congregation.

The car had to stop three times as it went through the Craggan grounds—twice for more guards to check their papers, once at the keeper's house for Ann Wynrame to get in. Alasdair got out to hold the door open for her. She was dressed in dark red tweeds, her hat a tiny gesture beside Mrs. Jardine's over-stocked flower-garden, her hair swept back across her forehead. She brushed past him, smiling fractionally, and climbed into the car. Alasdair got in beside her and closed the door. Without speaking, Wattie started off. Alasdair felt trapped and rescued at once. To cover his confusion, he looked out of the rear window. Hakonson was standing at the side of the road, looking fixedly after them. Then the car was round a corner, and the American was gone.

Another check at the bridge across the ravine, and the road was clear ahead. Down to Halmidary, still and withdrawn behind its Sunday curtains; northwards on to the open moor, with the black and white passing-place signs cutting a sharp line across a jumble of water-logged peat-hags. Ahead the watershed was slight, hardly definable; only the faintest of white lines at the meeting of moor and sky showed that far away the Arctic clouds were lying in wait.

Precise in his driving as in everything else, Wattie drove at a deliberate twenty miles an hour. They were not alone on the road. Ahead and behind, cars and vans were going in the same direction. The Reverend Aeneas was going to have an audience.

Wattie was slow, but he was also courteous. A horn hooted behind, and he pulled ponderously into the next passing-place, to allow the vehicle behind to overtake. Alasdair, fathoms deep in silence in the back seat, looked out to see a small red van pull past and accelerate away, the driver raising his hand as he went. Alasdair could read the name on the rear door—"Winesack's Supermarkets".

Just over the crest of the moor, where the little streams began to flow north, there was a quarry, littered with the evidence of former roadmaking—a derelict roadroller, a caravan with its roof blown in, and an acre of empty tar-drums. From it a path cut sharply away to the west, crossing the moor and the railway line on its far side and twisting into the hills beyond. Ten miles away along the path was Corrachan. They had come round two sides of a triangle with Halmidary at its apex. Alasdair looked at the path curiously. He couldn't spend all the afternoon in the car; here was a chance to escape.

"I think I'll get off here on the way back, Wattie," he said, "and walk over to Corrachan."

"It's a nice enough walk, right enough," the farmer commented. In the driving mirror Alasdair saw his face crease into a secret smile. What matter, he thought, I'm not getting out for the reason Wattie thinks. He looked sideways at Ann, whose face registered nothing. Then, beyond her, his eye caught a flash of metal in the furthest corner of the quarry. He looked again. The red van was sitting there.

*   *   *

Invermudale had once been a fishing port, smaller and less

hopeful than Rhintraid, but still a port with a pier and an ice-store, an inn at the pier-head and a row of mooring-buoys in the twisting channel of the Mudale river. Across the river, under the lee of a line of sandhills, the old house of Mudale crouched eyeless and gaunt, its windows empty and its roof sagging. On the hillside above, the bare fields ran up to the skyline, broken by long dykes of Caithness paving-stone.

The regatta was, in fact, in full swing. A confusion of cars and buses at the pier head suggested that the occasion was being a successful one. Half a dozen little dinghies were tacking back-wards and forwards against the current. The audience, large but obviously ignorant, was taking very little notice of them. But then, Alasdair realised, the occasion was what mattered, not the ostensible reason for the occasion. The promise of excite-ment was in the air, and everyone was well aware of it. The boats were only the overture; the play was still to come. They were, after all, incomers like himself, and now the natives were waiting for the thunderbolts to fall.

Two things dominated the scene. The one was the Inver-mudale Inn, a depressed building with dirty-white walls, and a faded notice proclaiming its possession of a seven-day licence and extolling its virtues as a fisherman's paradise. The word 'paradise' had apparently been deleted at one time in the past—probably in deference to the Reverend Aeneas—but it showed through the covering streak of black paint. Now, however, the inn was acting as a paradise for more than fishermen. As he watched, Alasdair saw at least a dozen men slip quietly through the side-door; their womenfolk, elaborately unconcerned with what was happening, walked on towards the pier.

There the second centre of attention was also in operation. The barrel-like figure of the Reverend Aeneas—absurdly reminiscent of some indulgent Catholic priest—was surrounded by several brethren of his own cloth, and a wider circle of respectful women. The blackness of the gathering, unrelieved by anything more colourful than the Reverend Aeneas' white collar, shouted at Alasdair as it dominated the forefront of the landscape. Around and beyond were the white sails of the dinghies, the waters and the sands, and the blues and greens of the Arctic sea. Far away two ships lay hull down to the north; high above gulls circled and swooped. But the darkness of the Reverend Aeneas controlled it all.

At the end of the pier the organisers of the regatta were clustered self-consciously, looking occasionally over their shoulders at the clerical batteries massed behind them. Some sort of salvo was clearly being prepared, for the Reverend Aeneas was clearing his throat and buttoning his black raincoat more tightly around him.

Wattie was unimpressed.

"The old hoodie crow," he muttered, "doesn't he know that there are at least three of his own congregation inside the bar at this very moment? Come on, Alasdair. We'll follow their example and hope that the minister notices us going." He turned towards the inn.

"You'll do no such thing, Wattie Jardine," said his wife, but without conviction. Alasdair paused irresolutely. It was Ann who settled the issue.

"Of course he will, Mrs. Jardine," she said. "You and I are going to walk over to these rocks and sit down to watch what goes on. I'm hardly respectably dressed by the standards of this prayer meeting."

Mrs. Jardine gave up. "But see you keep off the whisky," she flung at Wattie over her shoulder. Her husband, half-way to the bar door, paid no attention. Alasdair followed him.

It was one of the paradoxes of life in Scotland, that most God-fearing but godless of countries, that it was easier to get drunk on a Sunday than on any other day. The formalities were simple. Alasdair and Wattie signed an imposing register, thereby committing themselves to the statement that they were travellers in the course of a journey, and were in need of refreshment. Then, and at an hour when on the other six days of the week the bar would have been closed, they were able to elbow their way past the others—church members and all—who had had the same idea, and to force themselves on the attention of the two exhausted barmen.

Wattie, two whiskies in his hands, led the way to a corner beside the door and sat down. Alasdair, standing beside him, looked round the room. It was filled almost entirely with men in blue suits, respecting the day to the extent of drinking in the same clothes in which they had gone to church in the morning. A knot of yachtsmen, probably southerners from Dounreay, huddled together for protection at one end of the bar and talked rather too loudly. And beyond—Alasdair stiffened.

Naverack was sitting at the far end of the room, under the only window. There was a glass on the table in front of him, but he wasn't touching it. On his face there was a look Alasdair had seen before. A quick glance at the boy sitting beside the Professor was for confirmation only. Alasdair knew what he would see there, had seen it all before in a dozen sulky, half-beautiful student faces. The Professor of Entrepreneurial Ethics was at it again. Alasdair felt sorry for the young man in the too-new green fisherman's jersey.

Wattie pushed a whisky across the table to him. Alasdair picked it up and drank.

"That's better," Wattie chuckled. "You were nearly keeping me waiting."

"All right, all right, I'll get you another one," Alasdair said, gathering up the two empty glasses and making his way to the bar.

He had just collected the new drinks when a flash of green caught his eye. He looked up. The sulky young man was leaving—reluctantly. Another man was on the point of sitting down at Naverack's table. A very different sort of man, this. Short, broad, tough—not at all the sort of man for whom Alasdair would have expected Naverack to give up the boy in the green jersey. Alasdair felt his curiosity beginning to stir.

"Here you are. I'll be back in a minute," he said, handing Wattie the drinks. It took some time and some care, but eventually he managed to get close to Naverack's table, where, as he filled the pipe he had pulled out of a pocket, he was able to see the stranger more clearly.

The conversation was serious, low-voiced, and Alasdair could hear nothing of it. But he could see enough. The man was distinctive; a scar ran through one eyebrow, and two teeth were broken. A dangerous man to run across in the wrong circumstances. Not Naverack's type—not either of Naverack's types; not another administration man, and certainly not one of the Professor of Entrepreneurial Ethics' young men. Odd. Alasdair kept on watching.

The stranger pushed back his chair and pulled out a cigarette packet. As he put a cigarette to his lips, Naverack slipped a small package on to the table. The cigarette packet came down on top of it; then both were in the stranger's pocket, and he was opening a box of matches. Naverack paid no attention. The whole episode had taken no more than a second—only Alasdair had seen the wad of banknotes, wrapped around with paper, but with the ends showing.

Alasdair turned towards the window and stared hard out of it. Naverack was getting to his feet. He nodded to the stranger, and pushed his way through the room and out of the door. The man with the scar went over to the bar and bought a whisky. By the time he was back at his table Alasdair was at Wattie's side again.

The farmer looked curiously at him.

"Do you know that fellow?" he asked.

"No. But I used to know the man who just went out."

Wattie nodded and said nothing. He knew Alasdair well enough to realise that his past was not something to ask questions about. After a pause he looked at his watch.

"About time we were going. The wife will be getting angry."

Outside, religion and pleasure had met on the pier. But not in quite the way the Reverend Aeneas had expected. Wattie and Alasdair were just in time to see him being handed solicitously out of one of the dinghies, dripping wet. In the situation ecclesiastical dignity was difficult. Nor was the minister helped by hearing one of the yachtsmen refer to himself and his colleagues as fishers of men. Pointing accusingly at a length of rope, over which he had evidently stumbled, the Reverend

Aeneas beat a retreat—to meet, face to face, two of his own congregation coming out of the inn.

At the end of the pier Mrs. Jardine was talking to a woman wearing as notable a hat as her own. Wattie groaned at the sight.

"Old Mrs. Macvean from Sallachan," he whispered to Alasdair. "We'll not escape having to go and have tea with her. It's only ten minutes away in the car. Make an excuse if you can. She'll say a grace a quarter of an hour long just to make up for having come here this afternoon."

Forewarned, Alasdair escaped. Ann was half-way down the pier, and he made his way towards her. Mrs. Jardine shot a quick look after him, contemplated a fight, saw Wattie's face, and thought better of it.

"We'll be back in an hour and a half—no sooner. Wait for us here," Wattie muttered.

Ann turned as Alasdair came up to her side. She smiled quickly.

"The Jardines are off to have tea with that woman over there," Alasdair said quickly. "Wait ten minutes, and then we'll have an hour to ourselves."

Ann looked down. The tension was physical, overwhelming. Alasdair found himself puffing at a cigarette without being aware of having lit it. He watched the people within range, unable to believe that they did not realise what was happening.

Wattie's car moved slowly away along the road, passing the retreating minister and his convoy. The crowd was thinning fast. The afternoon's entertainment was over.

"I want to look at the sea," Ann said. "Can we walk down to the beach?"

Alasdair nodded. He didn't trust himself to speak.

Beyond the pier a cart-track led along the river bank towards the sea. Inside a quarter of a mile they were clear of the spectators, with only an agitated colony of terns as escort. Up against the sky, far above, a pair of fulmars wheeled and soared. Ann watched them, one hand holding her hat against the wind that rustled over the dunes from the sea. Alasdair walked carefully, a little after her, aware all the time of the people behind them.

The dunes grew higher. They came to an old fishing bothy, and the end of the track. The sound of the waves was louder now. They scrambled over a last ridge of soft sand, and looked out on to the Atlantic, blue and empty, except for the two ships far out to sea.

Ann stood watching for a long time. He saw her face grow remote, saw the happiness ebb out of it. All at once she turned and took hold of his hand, pulling him off the ridge and into the shelter of the dunes. Down amongst the marram grass she stopped, breathless, and swung round to look at his face. He put his hand on her shoulders. Her hat fell to the sand; the wind caught it and sent it rolling away out of his sight.

"My dear, my dear," she said. "So little time."

Afterwards, lying content on the hot sand, feeling the grains trickle between his fingers, he watched the snake of his conscience stir. This was involvement, dangerous involvement—dangerous for him, more dangerous still for Ann. That was bad; but it didn't worry him. There was something else he had to tell her.

"Ann," he said softly.

She opened her eyes, and rolled over until she could let her fingers run through his hair. He stretched up and kissed her hand.

"Yes," she said.

"There's a woman at the lodge——"

She laughed quietly.

"Mrs. Hakonson. I've seen her. When did you go to bed with her?"

"How did you know that?"

"I didn't. But she's quite a common type, and it seemed the obvious confession. Tell me."

He told her.

"I see," she said. "Now I know more about you. That's good."

Her fingers gripped his hair hard and pulled his head back. She leaned over and kissed him.

"Now leave her alone. Always."

After a long silence he spoke again.

"I think the police may suspect that I mistook the dead man in the river for her husband."

Her hand slowed, almost stopped. Then she continued stroking his hair.

"Why do you say that?"

"Obvious enough. Similarity of build for a start."

"But why should they worry about you?"

"I used to teach at Perth University. Cattanach knows that. The Hakonsons were at Perth last year. And——"

"That's enough." Ann sat up and smoothed her hair. "We don't know that the man was killed. Have the police said so?"

"No."

"Then wait until they do. And wait until they start asking questions."

Something in her voice made him look quickly at her.

"And then?" he said, buttoning up his shirt.

"Tell them the truth," Ann said, getting to her feet. She looked down at him, her face grave. "I don't want you hurt any more."

"What about us? When will I see you again?"

She looked away.

"I don't know. Wait." She picked up her hat and shook the sand out of it. "We must go. Wattie will be back soon."

CHAPTER SIX

"ARE you going across the hills, Alasdair?" Wattie asked over his shoulder.

The car was climbing up to the summit, and the quarry lay ahead, a dark slash on the face of the moor. If he was going to walk, he would have to get out very soon. He hesitated. Sitting in the car beside Ann was a suspended miracle, something that could go on for ever. He didn't want to leave her a second before he had to. But there were difficulties. It would look less blatant if he went over the hills.

Ann made up his mind for him.

"It's a good evening for a walk," she said. "I wish I could go with you."

The tone was dismissive; Alasdair took the hint.

"Let me off at the quarry, Wattie," he said. Then he remembered the van. He didn't want to meet anyone connected with Winesack. Winesack meant Naverack, and that was part of the dead past.

Suddenly he saw his chance. The quarry was only two hundred yards away, and a car was coming down the hill towards them. Wattie drew into a passing-place and waited for the car to come on.

"I'll just get out here," Alasdair said quickly, opening the door as he spoke.

There was a low embankment beside the road. He crossed it and dropped into the hollow beyond. The car passed, and Wattie moved on. He saw Ann looking at him out of the side window. And that, he thought, makes one thing more to explain away.

Wattie's car slid out of sight over the ridge, its sound hovering in the still air. Over the watershed another car came, accelerating away past him on its way to Invermudale. Something made him wait in the hollow, watching the quarry and the path beyond. Five minutes passed: ten. A buzzard wheeled past high above; a crow called harshly out of the peat hags. He kept his eyes on the path.

Half a mile away on the moor something was moving. He dropped and lay flat, praying that no cars would come along the road. The moving speck on the path came nearer, changed into a human figure, then into two, one walking behind the other. They passed out of sight under the rim of the knoll where the quarry lay. Taking his chance, Alasdair got up and sprinted along the side of the road towards the quarry. Fifty yards from it he flopped down behind a mossy boulder sticking out of the peat.

He was just in time. From the quarry came the sound of a starting motor. Slowly, the van came into sight. A pause, and then it was turning across his line of sight. It nosed out on to the road, accelerated, and disappeared over the crest in the direction of Halmidary.

Alasdair lay still and waited as the moor fell silent again. He had something to think about. He hadn't been able to make out the driver of the van, but his companion had been quite distinct. It was Thomson the policeman, in civilian clothes.

Thomson. Not a man whom he had ever liked. He liked him even less now. The policeman was a young man, narrow-mouthed and hard-eyed, with an undertow of his native Glasgow still clear in his speech. He talked too much in Alasdair's opinion, and in that of most people in the strath. Also, he was unmarried and not very sociable, and the strath liked its policeman to be approachable and established. Thomson was an outsider, almost a foreigner. He came from Glasgow and nowhere else; he was no Highlander who had grown up there and come back to his calf-ground to settle down. All of which made him a man to be suspected.

But suspected of what? Alasdair got to his feet and walked to the quarry. One set of wheel tracks only. The van had been there all afternoon. But why? What was going on in the hills?

Police work? Part of the Craggan security net? Deer poaching? An illicit still? He shrugged, and put his feet to the path. It was six o'clock, and there were ten miles to Corrachan.

As he walked, the moor began to rise in front of him into low hills. The path, crossing the railway, wound into them, taking long slanting lines up the shoulders, dropping down to cross shallow stony streams, but always heading westwards. Now and then, in damp patches, he could see fresh footmarks. An hour passed, an hour and a half. The road was far out of sight now, and the hills were getting steeper. Ahead, the path turned away from a north-pointing valley and made straight up the face of a long ridge. Once over that he would be half-way, looking down at a ruined pony stable beside a stream that ran into Loch Skiag. The slope was steep, and the sun was now so low that it only occasionally struck the path. It was in one of the patches of sunlight that he saw the spent match lying on the stones at his feet. He stooped and picked it up; it was fresh and dry, struck only a few hours before. So Thomson had been as far as this. Again he was puzzled, and apprehensive too. What was ahead? Or who?

Nearing the crest, he slowed. The skyline was dangerously open, even if he didn't know to what he was exposing himself. He looked round, telling himself as he did so that the whole idea was nonsense. But somehow, in the emptiness of the hills, it didn't feel like nonsense. He wasn't going to stay on the path. To his left the hill climbed higher, curving round to the west. He stepped off the path and turned across the face of the slope, keeping well under the crest.

Half a mile along he dropped to all fours, crawled to the top, and looked over. Below the sunlight was streaming into a wide corrie. The path fell into it in zig-zags, then made straight for the ruins of the stable. Alasdair started to search the corrie. If Thomson had been up to anything, this was the most likely place to find any traces of it. He took his time, for the flattening rays of the sun were throwing long shadows. He was glad that he had automatically brought his binoculars. The air was absolutely still. The sound of the burn in the corrie floated up to him, and the calls of the wading birds as they flickered from stone to stone. But there was no other sound, no sign of movement.

For all that, he was uneasy. The old stable had three of its walls still standing, and from the ridge he could not see what lay behind them. But the one remaining window looked straight towards his hiding-place, and there was something glittering behind its empty blackness. He lay still and watched. Rather than go down into the corrie, he began to plan a long detour to the south, keeping the ridge between himself and the stable. But for the moment he waited, without knowing quite what he expected to see. If Thomson had been working a still, then the equipment would be hidden somewhere in the hills. If he had been poaching, then he was unlikely to have left any carcasses in so obvious a place. Puzzled, but reluctant to go, Alasdair kept on looking.

Nothing happened. He inched forward to see down the near slopes of the corrie, feeling uncommonly foolish and exposed as he did so. Then he stopped. The glint in the stable window had gone. He lowered his head behind a bank of heather, and brought the binoculars carefully up. The glint reappeared, in the doorway this time, then vanished again in a rush of movement. And now a man was standing outside the stable. At the distance his features were indistinguishable in the shadow of his stalker's cap. But he was clearly on the alert. He moved quickly away from the wall, looking first one way and then the other. There was a revolver in his hand as he circled the stable, searching the hillside as he went. Alert, but hardly suspicious, Alasdair thought, watching the man go back into the ruins. Almost at once he came out again, carrying a bucket. He filled the bucket at the burn and went into the stable. This time he did not reappear.

Alasdair edged himself back over the ridge. Twenty feet below the summit he stood up and brushed the loose heather from his tweeds. Whatever else the stranger's presence meant, one thing was clear: Thomson and his companion had been to see him that afternoon. But why?

There wasn't much point in guessing. Besides, it was getting late, and now he would have an extra two miles to walk. He started off at top speed along the hillside, glad to stretch his legs after his long lie in the heather. He was going so fast, his eyes on the ground just ahead, that he never saw Gruar until he was right on top of him. He stumbled to a halt, panting, and eyed the assistant factor without friendliness. Enough complications already; and Gruar was one complication that recurred too often.

Gruar got to his feet and looked up the hillside. Then he raised his right arm and signalled. As Alasdair watched, a second man, dressed in an anonymous battle-dress, came down from the ridge, giving a thumbs-up signal as he came.

"Right this time," he said to Gruar. "Jim's staying up there to watch. The man we're looking for is in a broken-down stable just over this hill. Six foot at least, wearing a brown tweed suit. We can't make out his face, but he's carrying a revolver."

"Is that right?" Gruar shot the question quickly at Alasdair.

"Yes. I can't add anything, but I certainly saw the revolver." Gruar nodded to the other man.

"Good enough, Fred. We'd better put a message through. Is Jim all right?"

"Yes. I'll go back to him as soon as I can."

Fred looked at Alasdair as he spoke, then sideways at Gruar.

"You'd better come with us, Alasdair," Gruar said slowly.

"I'm on my way to Corrachan—that way," Alasdair said, pointing westwards.

Gruar shook his head. Alasdair saw Fred's hand slide quietly into his pocket.

"No," Gruar said. "Come with us. I'm interested to know just why you've turned up here."

*   *   *

A mile away down the valley, at the end of a rough track, two Landrovers were sitting. One was fitted with a wireless transmitter.

"Get on to base," Gruar said to Fred. "Report success and give the map reference of that stable. Tell base to send out a relief team of two in the second wireless truck. Warn them that the man is armed. Clear?"

"Yes."

"When the relief turns up you and Jim can come back in this truck. I'm going on now. You'd better get back to Jim."

Fred looked doubtful, and glanced at Alasdair. Gruar grinned and shook his head. Then he turned to the second truck, signing Alasdair to follow.

"Food, Alasdair," he said.

Fred trudged off back up the valley. Gruar perched on the tailboard of the Landrover and watched him.

"On second thoughts, talk first and food second," he said. "Just what were you doing up there?"

He listened in silence as Alasdair told the story, from the moment he had left Wattie's car at the quarry. When Alasdair had finished, Gruar got down and squatted on his heels in the heather. He picked up a grass stem and chewed at it.

"This is where we start from," he said at last. "For the last eighteen months Russian agents have been getting in and out of Dounreay. We have our eyes on three or four of the Dounreay staff who are probably passing on information. We're pretty certain that the agents come by this strath, and that interests us a lot more than any conference. Particularly as two technicians slipped out of Dounreay last October and turned up in Russia a fortnight later. They were seen getting into a car at Invermudale, and that was the last report we ever got."

"How do I know that you and these two others are British Security?" Alasdair asked. The vague menaces were beginning to twist into shape, and he was uneasily aware that his own position was none too clear.

"You don't," Gruar said flatly. "But if you've any sense you'd better believe it. There's always that dead man in the river."

Alasdair looked narrowly at him.

"You know I had nothing to do with that," he said.

"Not quite. I don't think, if you'd killed him, that you would have been fool enough to take me right to the body. Inspector Cattanach might think differently, though."

"Is that a threat?"

Gruar took out a packet of cigarettes and tossed one over to Alasdair.

"No. No threat. But the Inspector will be starting serious enquiries tomorrow, for the Procurator-Fiscal is getting anxious. Then he'll be asking questions about people's movements on Friday night, and about possible motives. Are you going to tell him that you knew Hakonson?"

"Yes. Why not?"

"No reason at all. I hope you tell the Inspector everything that might help him."

Alasdair struck a match and sheltered it in his cupped hands whilst he lit his cigarette.

"Was the dead man a Russian?" he asked.

"All I know is that he had some slivers of insulated wire in his pocket. I picked up the same sort of wire in the conference room at Craggan, and with it two staples that have been identified as Russian-made. That's enough to go on just now."

"And the man across the hill in the stable?"

"Another Russian agent, probably. A pity we didn't spot him before you turned up. Somebody must be bringing him food up there."

"Meaning what?"

"Meaning just that we could have eliminated you from the list of possibilities on that score."

Alasdair nodded slowly.

"I get the point. You want me to talk?"

"Precisely. Not everything. If you've been making a pass at Wynrame's wife, that's your business—only next time cover your traces a bit better. But I'll hear anything else you've got to say."

Alasdair hesitated. The position was equivocal. He wasn't being accused, he wasn't being taken into collaboration; he was simply being made to show his hand completely. Something very like this had happened to him at Perth, and he had promised himself that he wouldn't be caught again. Crossrig had made him talk. Gruar wasn't going to.

Gruar read the look on Alasdair's face. He twisted quickly to his feet and stood looking down at his companion. Alasdair, legs dangling over the tailboard of the Landrover, stared back.

"Look," Gruar said. "I've told you that I'm not a policeman. If you killed that man, don't tell me, for I don't want to know. That's Cattanach's business. But there are some things you can help with. Get in my way, and you'll be hurt."

"Suppose I'm a Russian agent myself?" said Alasdair.

"Then I'm not in very much danger. Russian agents aren't encouraged to go in for gun-work unless absolutely necessary. I should think your instructions, if you are a Russian agent, are to say as little as possible and get away as soon as possible. So go ahead. You won't get very far."

"Two men went to the stable earlier today," Alasdair said. It was time to come off the fence. The threats weren't important. What was important, and unexpected, was that he found himself anxious to stay in the picture. This was another kind of involvement, and one that he didn't want to run away from.

"Go on," said Gruar, stubbing out his cigarette.

"One of the two was a stranger. He parked a van belonging to Winesack's Supermarkets on the Invermudale road this afternoon, and picked it up again just as I left the road."

"And who was with him?"

"Thomson the Rhintraid policeman—in plain clothes."

Gruar showed no surprise. He pulled a notebook out of his pocket and opened it.

"Yes. Thomson was off duty this afternoon. And you left Craggan in Jardine's car and went to Invermudale. So did Professor Naverack. Professor and Mrs. Hakonson stayed at Craggan. President Crossrig has been working in his room all day. Mrs. Wynrame was at Invermudale with you"—he hesitated fractionally before going on—"and her husband went out on the hill early this morning."

"I'll tell you what Naverack was doing at Invermudale," said Alasdair. "He passed a wad of banknotes to a man in the hotel."

Gruar was alert at once.

"What sort of man? Describe him."

He wrote down Alasdair's description.

"So. Naverack, Winesack: Winesack's van, Thomson the policeman: Naverack, a stranger, money. Interesting. Are you sure Thomson was at the stable?"

"He certainly went along that path. I found traces of some-one having used it today. Where could he have been going but the stable?"

Gruar nodded.

"Probably you're right. We'll see. Anything else?"

Alasdair hesitated.

"If Cattanach's wanting to find motives, and if he really does think that the dead man could have been mistaken for Hakonson, then I'm going to have to tell him that there's one person who could have had a motive for doing the killing."

"Who?"

"Myself. I was once Mrs. Hakonson's lover, not so very long ago."

"Awkward," said Gruar. "But not unique." He flicked over the pages of his book. "I'm told that she has a good deal of money of her own, that she's Hakonson's third wife, that at least two men in America have been divorced on account of her, and that her husband very politely appears to ignore her behaviour. You wouldn't know why, would you?"

"Not really. He must have known what she was up to at Perth—two professors and a warden, without counting lesser game like me. The money may be a consideration, but if I had to guess I'd say that he married her with his eyes closed, and now he can't lose face with himself."

"A classic murder situation," Gruar said, walking round to the front door of the truck. "The only trouble is that it's the wrong way round. What about the woman?"

Alasdair shrugged.

"I'm the one she wants this week. She's sure it's genuine this time. She always is sure. That's the trouble with her sort, whether you do what they want or whether you don't. Give her a month and she'll be after someone else. Just now she's a damned nuisance. But I'm sorry for Hakonson."

"There are worse compensations than money," Gruar said. "Also, I'm told he's been round at Wynrame's house on three or four occasions these last few days."

Alasdair, standing on the edge of a vast emptiness, said nothing.

After a moment's silence Gruar went on.

"Come back to the main point. Could you have mistaken the dead man for Hakonson?"

"No. The build is much the same, but that's about all."

"Neither could I. Still, the dead man does remind me of someone else here. I saw the resemblance fleetingly, and now I can't pin it down. If I knew that, we might be on the track of something."

Alasdair said nothing. He remembered the two pictures of the mountain valley. Hakonson mightn't look like the dead man, but there was a link between him and Ann Wynrame. That wasn't something to speak about; it wasn't even something to think about.

Gruar lifted a packet of sandwiches and a flask out of the car.

"Right. Food now. Then I'll drive you home," he said.

Alasdair picked up a sandwich, suddenly aware that he was very hungry. Gruar watched him.

"One last thing," he said, as he poured coffee from the flask. "You're involved now, whether you want it or not, but don't go around imagining you know everything that's going on. So far you've been mixed up in some episodes that interest me quite a lot. It may be just a coincidence, but I'd be a fool to assume that. I've got a job to do, and I mean to do it. The chances are pretty high that anyone getting in the way will end up by being hurt—and that applies even to innocent people."

*   *   *

By the time the relief Landrover appeared they had finished eating. The sun was tumbling towards the edge of the rolling hills. Midges hovered and settled in the evening air, but Alasdair let them be. Stiffness was creeping into his bones, and he felt tired. He was glad when Gruar produced a flask; the whisky tasted raw and cruel, but he forced it down.

The track wound southwards through the hills towards Craggan. Gruar, pushing the Landrover hard over the rough surface, talked about fishing, about stalking, about keepers and their habits. Alasdair answered his questions in monosyllables. One kind of tension was being replaced by another.

"That Mannlicher at Craggan—have you ever used it?" Gruar asked, as they climbed over a last ridge and saw Craggan lying below amongst its trees.

"No. I haven't fired a gun since I came here," Alasdair replied.

"It looks a good weapon. Wynrame had it when we met him at the wire bridge, hadn't he?"

"Yes."

"Did he have it earlier in the day?"

"Not when I saw him in Halmidary. But he couldn't have had it. Don't you remember that Naverack had left it on the hall table at the lodge?"

"You're right. Wynrame said he picked it up there before going out into the woods."

Gruar fell silent. Alasdair made no move to keep up the conversation. The Landrover slid down a slope on to the road.

"Where do you want to go?" Gruar asked. "Corrachan or your cottage?"

"The cottage," Alasdair replied. He didn't want to wake up and find himself alone in the hills. For one day at least, it would be comforting to be back within sight and sound of other people. And that, he thought wryly, was a change.

Gruar turned the machine towards Halmidary, slowed to get clearance from a figure in the shadows beside the road, and drove into the village in a renewed silence. He stopped opposite the post-office, and Alasdair got out. Out of the corner of his eye he could see the curtains stir in old Mrs. Chisholm's sitting-room across the road.

"You'd better go back to Corrachan tomorrow," Gruar said. "Stay pretty close until you get a message. And if Cattanach asks you any questions my advice is to tell him the truth. I can't shield you, and I won't shield you, if you're involved in that man's death. Good night."

The exhaust blared, and the Landrover accelerated away up to the hotel; Mrs. Chisholm's curtains twitched back into place. By the time Gruar had turned back towards Craggan Alasdair was halfway up the path to his cottage. He was angry, then he was frightened; the anger was hollow, the fear was self-pity; most of all, he was just plain tired.

He went through the hole in the dyke, opened the back door of the cottage, and let himself in. In the kitchen dust was beginning to gather. He pulled off his shoes, threw his jacket towards a peg on the wall, and sat down in the armchair. The weariness came flooding up over him, and it took an enormous effort to get to his feet again. Better to go to bed and sleep properly. He went through to the bedroom, flung back the cover on the bed, and changed into his pyjamas. Outside the sky was red with the last of the setting sun. He pulled the window wide open, and turned to go to bed.

A thought checked him, and he went back into the kitchen, took down a torch from the shelf and flashed it towards the bookcase. The book he wanted wasn't where he had left it. It wasn't on the shelf above. It wasn't on the shelf below. He stood back and wondered, playing the torch from shelf to shelf. The first shelf he had gone to was fractionally unfamiliar-looking. The books were bulging forwards, looking bigger than they should. He pulled half a dozen of them away, and the reason became plain. The book he wanted had got pushed behind, and was lying flat against the back of the shelf. He hadn't left it like that.

He took stock of the room. Now that he was suspicious, he could see a dozen inconsistencies glaring at him. The clock was slightly off straight; the ashes in the fireplace had been stirred;

one drawer of the dresser was not quite shut. Someone had been searching the house.

Five minutes' search was enough to convince him that nothing valuable had been taken. Whoever had been through the house must have been looking for something specific. Was it the police? Or Wynrame, smelling intrigue and looking for non-existent letters? Or Gruar's men, taking advantage of his absence with their chief? Or—what if something had been brought in, not taken out? A tape recorder, a microphone, or what?

He switched the torch out and stood by the window. It was unlikely to be the police. Without a search warrant that would be dangerous folly, and the public was not quite as impressed with its police nowadays as it had once been. But the other possibilities? He stood for a moment wondering, then gave it up, and went to bed. The waters were swirling deep and strong again.

CHAPTER SEVEN

"I'm going to start asking questions," Inspector Cattanach said, turning to look straight at Gruar. "That man hasn't been identified, and the Fiscal won't wait any longer."

Gruar lay back and stared out of the window of the police car at the birch trees sliding past.

"I'm not surprised," he said. "Are you beginning today?"

"Just so, just so. It's Monday now, and the Fiscal was after me this morning."

"What exactly is worrying him?"

"Murder—or so he thinks." Cattanach's voice was heavily non-committal. At the wheel Sergeant Ross stared rigidly ahead. Gruar said nothing. They were passing Loch Beannachd; beyond the Sergeant's head he could see the railway bridge at Halmidary.

"We can't prove anything," Cattanach went on after a long pause. "It could have been murder, though. If it was, then we'll have to find out what everyone at Craggan was doing on Friday night—and some other things besides."

"The man may have been a foreign agent," said Gruar. "I suppose you've thought of that?"

"And why wouldn't we think of it?" Cattanach retorted. "But that's not quite the point. Murder is murder, and I'm not having it happening here. I want to know who did it; the Fiscal wants to know too."

Gruar watched the Inspector's growing anger without enthusiasm. Law and order was one thing; the closed circle of the strath and its people was another. There would be complications if Cattanach pressed too hard—and complications were just what he wanted to avoid for the next forty-eight hours.

"I think the man was a Russian spy," he said. "But that's no reason why he should have been killed. On the whole spies don't get killed. So why should this man be killed? Who would kill a complete stranger—which he seems to have been?"

"There's a dead body, and we can't ignore that," said Cattanach from behind a cloud of blue smoke. His voice was obstinate. "I'm not saying that he was killed on purpose. But he could have been killed by mistake."

"And that means you've got your eye on Macvartney," Gruar said. The car slowed as Sergeant Ross threaded his way through the jumble of vehicles outside the Halmidary hotel. Cattanach nodded. He remained silent until they were across the railway line and heading up the Craggan road.

"Mind you," the Inspector said at last, "if we could identify the body and discover some motive for a deliberate murder, then I'd gladly think again. But meantime I find it a bit peculiar that Macvartney should have been about on Friday night, and that this should happen just when people from his old University turn up at Craggan. That's what I'm going on, for a start. And that's why I'm off up to Corrachan to ask Macvartney some questions. He was sleeping at Halmidary last night, but went away back to Corrachan before we could catch him."

"Are you going to question anyone else?" Gruar asked.

"Yes, indeed." The Inspector pulled out his notebook. "When do you think I could see the Hakonsons, Crossrig and Naverack?"

"Tomorrow, not today," Gruar said promptly. "I gather there will be a break in the conference tomorrow afternoon, if things keep up to schedule. Tonight they will be working late. I'll find out the best time for you. Do you remember, by the way, that I was wondering about Wynrame and the deer rifle?"

"The man was drowned; he wasn't shot." There was a touch of irritation in Cattanach's voice.

"The rifle is important, for all that. You could do worse than ask everyone at Craggan to try to remember if they saw it on Friday. Something was going on in the grounds that night—remember the stone in the road?"

"You're suspecting Wynrame, then?"

"I'm not saying that," Gruar retorted. "But Macvartney's not the only one that needs thinking about."

Cattanach looked sharply at him. Then he smiled and put his notebook away. The car swung round the corner by the bridge and plunged into the shade of the Craggan woods.

"It's not all that easy remembering that we've got different jobs to do here," the Inspector said, relighting his pipe. "Is your side under control?"

"So far, so good," replied Gruar. "But I'll be a lot happier when this collection are off my hands."

A man came out of the trees and waved the car to a halt. Sergeant Ross handed over his police pass. The man studied it, then peered into the back of the car. He saw Gruar, and stood back.

"All clear, sir," he said. "Nothing to report."

Ross drove on.

"I'll let you off at the fork," Cattanach said. "We'll go straight to Corrachan to talk to Macvartney. Then on the way down I'll have a word with Wynrame and his wife, if they're in. We should——"

He broke off as Gruar tapped his arm and pointed. Ahead, a car was coming out of the Craggan branch of the road. As they watched, it turned towards Corrachan.

"If I were you, I'd give it half an hour before I went to see Macvartney," said Gruar, opening the car door.

"Why? Who was in that car?"

"That was Mrs. Hakonson—alone. If you ask Macvartney, he'll probably tell you that she and her husband spent a year at Perth University recently. You pointed out yourself that Hakonson is very similar in build to the dead man."

*   *   *

Alasdair sat in the boat looking at the broken oar. The light westerly wind was sending the wavelets chopping against the stern; slowly the bow dropped round and the clumsy craft, designed for drifting downwind with a couple of fishermen aboard, began to lurch away from the shore. Time to do something, if he wasn't to spend the rest of the afternoon in the middle of the loch. He stood up, took the remaining good oar, and poled the boat back to the golden beach.

The bow grounded with a hiss. He jumped out, and pulled the boat up behind him. The sands were soft and clean, no sodden sea-mud, but a multitude of individual grains, each bright and clear and separate. He pulled off his heavy hill shoes and sat down. Around him there was nothing of man at all. Only the sand, and the meadow grass behind, along the twisting banks of the burn. And beyond that only the heather, and a soaring hawk, and the chatter of the wading birds. He was as far away as he could be. Corrachan was out of sight round a headland, the road to Craggan was lost in a fold of the hills. Here at the top end of Loch Skiag, beside the stream where the salmon would come to spawn in the autumn, was the end of his road.

He lay back on the sand and stared up at the shimmering face of Creag an Lochain. The sun was hot, the wind was light, he was completely alone. He watched the wind bounce off Creag an Lochain, sending the water scudding in a dozen different directions at once. Easy enough, if he looked long enough, to imagine some underwater turbulence, to construct some hypothetical monster to explain it, and then to become convinced by his own delusions. A water horse, an *each uisge*, perhaps, or a gigantic bull with flippers and a shark's tail, or a Naverack with a unicorn's horn. Not a place for too much imagination. He tried to think what it must look like in winter, under snow and ice, and failed.

But the oar had broken. That was the flaw in the crystal. The wood was sound enough; this wasn't a case of old age or rottenness. The oar had hit something beneath the surface—something so heavy and solid that the oar had snapped under the impact.

He sat up and eyed the water speculatively. Highland lochs were liable to contain many things—old cooking stoves, rusty

G

baths, derelict motor cars. The likelihood of finding such things at the head of Loch Skiag, however, was small. That would have required more determination to conceal rubbish than the Highlander normally showed. There was a chance, but only a remote one, that the oar had struck an abandoned mooring-buoy, or the stump of a post.

The wind died away into nothingness. In front of him the loch stretched blue and still. The temptation was irresistible. He stripped off his clothes and waded in. The coldness was electric, making his heart race and sending every limb tingling. He broke into a racing crawl, dived into the depths of the loch, and came up to break water, panting, but with breath enough to shout and hear the echoes roll back at him from Creag an Lochain.

Treading water, he circled slowly, trying to locate his position in relation to the shore on either hand. The boat had been less than thirty yards out when the oar had broken, and in no great depth of water, for he had been able to use the other oar as a pole. He dived once, groping, and came up spluttering. He dived again, and his hands struck something metallic. He felt for a hold, failed to get one, and had to come up for air. A careful look to mark his position, and then he was making for the bank.

Ashore, he shook himself, dug a cigarette out of his pockets, and stretched out in the shelter of the tall grass to dry in the sunshine. Whatever was lying under the water in the loch was a shadow on innocence, a reminder of the world outside. He was angry that it should be there at all, angry with himself for wanting to discover what it was; but he knew that he was going to find out.

Once dressed, he pushed the boat out again. Using the remaining oar to steer, he drifted stern first towards the spot where he had touched the mysterious object. He lay full length along a seat, put his head over the gunwale, and watched. The sunlight was strong, and he had no difficulty in making out the bottom of the loch—a flat floor of mud, covered with a sparse carpet of weed and water-grass. From time to time small trout darted in and out of his vision. The lapping of the water on the boat's side came from far away, from a different world. Once he stiffened at the sight of something glistening ahead, then relaxed when it turned out to be a beer bottle, relic of some fisherman's picnic lunch.

Then, when he had almost stopped expecting anything, he saw them—two large oil drums, floating eighteen inches beneath the surface, anchored to the bottom by a rope with two weights attached. He leaned further over. There was writing on the ends of the drums, but he couldn't make it out properly. From one end of the securing rope a thin wire ran shorewards. He followed its course for a little, but the mud had swirled over and around it, and he soon lost sight of it.

The wind stirred uneasily, and the boat swept past the sunken drums. Alasdair stood up and poled back to the beach. It was possible, he told himself, that somebody had once kept a motor launch on the loch, and that these were empty drums, dumped out of sight from a feeling of tidiness. But he didn't believe it; the drums didn't look old. And if they were new, why were they not simply lashed down at the edge of the beach?

He tied the boat to a rock, stowed the oars and rowlocks, and prepared to walk back to the lodge. The Corrachan rifle—a Mannlicher identical with that at Craggan—was lying in the bows of the boat. He picked it up. His fishing rod could stay. The Mannlicher, on the other hand, gave him a feeling of security, when he remembered his talk with Gruar the night before, and the stranger with the revolver crouching in the stable a few miles away.

*   *   *

The open door of the lodge caught his eye as he came up the path from the suspension bridge across the Blackwater. It had been closed when he left in the morning. Frowning, he changed course towards it. More trouble ahead, he sensed.

There was. Inside the living-room, under the heads of the

great royal stags and the pencilled records of famous kills, Erica Hakonson was sitting.

Alasdair set the Mannlicher down carefully on the table and looked at her without speaking. Erica, hands peacefully folded in her lap, looked back at him. One finger only was moving, beating ceaselessly against the tiny watch on her wrist.

"You've been a long time," she said.

"I told you I didn't want to see you again."

She laughed and leaned back in her chair. He could see the scar on her ear, could see the tensing line of her body. But this time he wasn't going to be caught. He picked up the Mannlicher, released the magazine, and emptied the bullets one by one on to the table.

"You've got to see me," Erica said. The sudden note of desperation in her voice pleased him.

"Why?" he asked, lining the lead-nosed bullets side by side on the green baize.

She stood up in one fluid movement and put a hand on his shoulder. He twisted out of reach, his elbow knocking the bullets down as he did so.

"You were glad enough to have me last year." Her voice was bitter now.

"Along with half a dozen others. And what about your collection across the Atlantic?"

"That's different. It's all washed up now. Can't you get it into your head that I'm asking you—you—you?" Her voice rose and cracked.

Alasdair began to set the bullets in line again.

"You've got a man of your own. Go back to him," he said flatly.

Her laugh was less controlled this time.

"Him? If he'd any guts he'd have horsewhipped me long before this. And if he thinks he's going to——"

She stopped, suddenly cunning.

"If he thinks he's going to—what?" Alasdair asked, the last bullet in his hand.

Erica looked hard at him, her hysteria vanishing under a wave of calculation.

"If he thinks he's going to throw me over for that game-warden's wife, then he's going to find out just who can move fastest."

The bullet slipped through Alasdair's fingers. He took hold of Erica's shoulders and began to shake her. She relaxed and fell forward, then clung to him. He pushed her away, hard. She stumbled backwards against the wall, one hand at her throat, her eyes wide with the success of her thrust.

"You'd better explain that, quick," Alasdair said, putting his hand on the butt of the rifle.

Erica straightened up, sensing her chance, feeling the initiative pass back to her. She smoothed her hair before she spoke.

"I'm telling you, that's how it is. Leif is hooked up with that Mrs. Wynrame. You like her too, don't you? He was across there last evening, late on, and that's enough. When I get back home, it's Reno for me. That phoney Viking's been scared yellow for his own skin ever since we got here, and now I aim to get out."

"I don't believe you," said Alasdair mechanically, bending down and picking up the fallen bullet.

Erica, in full control now, sat down again.

"Keep your eyes open—or ask Wynrame himself. He's been opening his mouth about it. I reckoned something was going on, but he put me right in the picture. So what about it?"

"About what?"

"Don't be so dumb. I'm asking you, Alasdair. Come with me. Once I'm through in Reno we can get married, if you want it that way."

"It wouldn't work. You couldn't keep your claws off anything in trousers that happened to be available," he said savagely.

For an instant she looked lost and crushed. Then she smiled uncertainly.

"Don't be so sure," she said. "Why not chance it?"

"Try someone else," Alasdair said shortly. He was still falling through the enormous chasm she had opened up in front of him. Slowly a picture was beginning to form. There had been a monumental miscalculation somewhere, but the result was clear—he had been played for a sucker. Why had Ann done it? The answer came quickly: because Wynrame was a spy, and she was a spy too—any other way it didn't make sense. Somehow it had fitted their plans to use him. All at once he felt very tired.

Erica was talking again. She slid out of the chair and came up behind him, leaning forward against his arm so that he could feel the pressure of her breasts. He twisted sharply away.

"Who do you reckon I'd try?" she was saying. "Old man Crossrig never knew how, and your sidekick Naverack is more interested in pretty boys. Don't pass it up, Alasdair. You may think I'm a bitch and nothing else, but you're wrong this time."

She was standing in front of him now, her hands held out. Wearily he turned his head away. The stags on the wall, their goitrous marble eyes glistening in the sunlight, looked down indifferently. This was his ivory tower, and all its doors were open.

"It wouldn't work. I've nothing to give you. There's nothing left between us. You must——"

He broke off. There was a shadow on the floor, and Erica was staring wide-eyed past him.

"Good afternoon, Mr. Macvartney," came the voice of Inspector Cattanach. "The door was open, so I just came in. I'd like to have a little talk with you."

It took Alasdair a moment to realise the implications. His first thought was that this was a chance of getting rid of Erica. Only when he saw the Inspector's glance take in the rifle and the neat row of bullets did he begin to feel uneasy. But there was nothing to do but play the scene out. What conclusions Cattanach would draw were beyond his control.

The Inspector remained standing in the doorway, his peaked cap in his hand. The silence was palpable. Erica, her face pale, was deep in some private perplexity. At last Alasdair could stand it no longer.

"Of course, Inspector. Whenever you like. Have you met Mrs. Hakonson? Her husband's staying at Craggan this week."

It was, in the circumstances, an over-long speech, and he knew it. He had let the initiative slip out of his hands. But he wanted Erica away before the Inspector began to ask his questions.

Cattanach, the silence broken, was all politeness.

"Pleased to meet you, Mrs. Hakonson. My name is Cattanach, of the local police. In fact, I was going to call on you and your husband at Craggan tomorrow. You won't be from home, I'm hoping."

He laid his cap on the table beside the rifle, and sat down in one of the armchairs.

"Do you mind if I smoke my pipe?" he said to Erica, pulling a tobacco pouch from his pocket and unrolling it.

Erica came to life suddenly. Alasdair saw her lips close into a narrow, bitter line. Then her whole face changed; by some deliberate interior effort she wiped her expression blank. Now she was the simple, uncomplicated, transatlantic sex-machine again, and she gave Cattanach the full benefit of it.

"You go right ahead, Inspector. I'm going back to Craggan. Leif and I will be pleased to meet you tomorrow, if he's not in conference. See you soon, Alasdair."

Cattanach made no move to stop her as she walked out of the door. A minute later the sound of a car engine came from behind the byre. Cattanach went to the door and watched. When the noise had died away he turned back into the room.

"I've got Sergeant Ross out in the car," he said, "but I'll not call him in. You'd maybe prefer to talk a bit without anyone taking notes."

"If notes mean a sworn statement, then you're right," Alasdair said. "Now perhaps you'll tell me what all this is about."

"That's reasonable," Cattanach said mildly, lighting his pipe, his red face glowing through the blue smoke. "Yes, indeed, that's reasonable. I've been reading your statement about finding this body on Friday night. Yon painted lassie from America was worried—why?"

The attack took Alasdair by surprise. He fingered one of the bullets before replying.

"She's afraid," he said shortly.

"Afraid of what?"

Alasdair stared straight at the Inspector.

"Afraid she won't ever go to bed with me again."

"Indeed, Mr. Macvartney? And will she?"

"No."

"But she has done before?"

"Yes."

"When?"

"A year ago—at Perth."

"Just so, just so. Well, it's a relief to learn that the pleasures of fornication can pall. I wouldn't be knowing myself."

Cattanach got up out of his chair and began to prowl round the room.

"So," he said over his shoulder, "you could have a reason— or maybe you once had a reason—to dislike Professor Hakonson? And of course you have a grievance against yon unpleasant man Naverack, and even against President Crossrig, if my information is correct."

"You've found out a good deal," Alasdair said grimly.

"Ach, we have our ways. Was it because of Mrs. Hakonson that you were sacked from Perth University?"

"Mainly."

"A pity, that. The women are a difficulty sometimes. My own uncle lost his professorship, but that was just the drink."

He picked up the Mannlicher and squinted along the sights.

"You'll be wondering just what I'm after," he said, aiming at the centre of a cobweb suspended between the antlers of an enormous stag.

"I'm not a fool," Alasdair said shortly.

"I never thought it. So you'll be thinking that I suspect you of having a hand in the death of that man who was found in the river?"

"Was the man killed?"

Cattanach lowered the rifle slowly and shrugged.

"If I was sure of that you'd be down at the police station in Dalbreck by now. There hasn't been a murder in this county in the last thirty years, and I'm not having an unexplained one now. That's why I want you to tell me just what you were doing last Friday night."

Alasdair told him. Cattanach listened carefully.

"Some points there," he said when Alasdair had finished. "You didn't meet Professor Naverack in the Craggan grounds?"

"No. I met Mrs. Hakonson on my way to the farm, and then afterwards Crossrig, Hakonson and Wynrame—and of course Mrs. Wynrame was at the farm."

"Well, that's all easily enough checked."

"There was the person Mrs. Wynrame and I saw crossing the path," Alasdair added.

"Unidentified. That could mean something. You didn't see this stone that ditched Mrs. Jardine's car?"

Alasdair shook his head.

"No. But I didn't pass MacCrossich's ditch anyway."

"I suppose you had time enough, between passing the Halmidary level-crossing and arriving at the farm, to go down through the woods to the place where the body was found?"

Alasdair smiled without amusement. He picked up the bullets and put them in his pocket.

"You wouldn't expect me to tell you if I had gone, would you? But you're right enough—time enough to go down, kill a man, and get back to the road. If you used a stopwatch, you'd probably find that I had time too between taking Mrs. Wynrame home and meeting Mr. Gruar and the others at the bridge. The only complication is that I didn't. If I had killed the man I'd have taken good care not to let his body be found so soon afterwards."

"Maybe." Cattanach fingered his moustache. "My southern colleagues tell me that criminals don't always think that way."

"Are you going to suspect anyone else?"

"Everybody." Cattanach's laugh lasted a shade too long.

"And nobody. Just now I'm only asking questions, and I've got a lot more to ask. For instance, can you confirm that Wynrame had a rifle like this when you met him at the bridge?"

"Yes. Anything else?"

Cattanach considered for a moment.

"No. Not unless you can think of any incident on Friday night that might help me."

Alasdair hesitated. At the back of his mind there was an awareness that something had been unusual, anomalous. He groped for it, missed. He shook his head.

"Nothing I can think of."

Cattanach picked up his cap and walked towards the door.

"In that case I'll be going. Time I was back in Dalbreck."

"Just a minute, Inspector," said Alasdair. "Would you mind telling me just what sort of a case you think you might get against me?"

"No," Cattanach said. "I won't do that. But I'll tell you this much. If the dead man had been Professor Hakonson, you'd have more than questions to answer. What I've seen here today makes that clear."

"But the man wasn't Professor Hakonson."

"Agreed. Still, mistakes are easy enough in the half-dark."

"I see. So it would help me if you could identify the dead man?"

Cattanach snorted.

"It would help everybody."

"Why not ask Mr. Gruar and his security team at Craggan, then? Or have you?" said Alasdair maliciously.

For the first time Cattanach showed signs of anger.

"That's none of your business," he said. "As far as you're concerned Mr. Gruar is Mr. MacAra's assistant. Just remember that."

He turned on his heel and walked out. Alasdair followed, and stood watching him cross to his car. The interview had been inconclusive, almost abortive, but at least Cattanach now knew what had happened in the past. For himself, he knew what he had already presumed, that he was a person to be suspected, even before it was clear that a crime had been committed. It didn't seem very important beside what Erica had told him about Ann.

*   *   *

Half a mile on Sergeant Ross pulled the police car into a passing-place. Cattanach leaned forward, saw what was approaching, and swore under his breath.

"Get right off the road," he ordered Ross. "Here's Mr. MacAra in his shooting brake, and you know what his driving is like."

The brake halted in a cloud of dust, gravel crunching under its tyres. MacAra was driving, with Gruar beside him.

The factor lowered his window and leaned out.

"It's a fine day, Inspector. Is Macvartney at Corrachan?"

"Indeed yes, Mr. MacAra. I've been having a talk with him."

"Which is just what I'm off to do myself," MacAra said, "so I'll be getting out of your way."

Gruar opened his door quickly and got out.

"I'd like to speak to the Inspector," he said to MacAra. "I'll walk on to the lodge after you. It isn't far."

He stood back amongst the heather until the cloud of dust had subsided and MacAra was out of sight round the next bend. Then he walked over to the police car and leaned against its bonnet. Cattanach climbed out and stood beside him. Pulling a piece of paper from his pocket, Gruar handed it to the Inspector. Cattanach took out a pair of spectacles and read, grunting to himself as he did so.

"I see. So McGlashan the poacher was seen at Inverness around lunchtime, in a black Chevrolet, with two other men. And what's important about that?"

"Do you think he'll come to the strath tonight?"

"Your guess is as good as mine on that, Mr. Gruar. Anyway, I've more important things to think about. What's one more poaching raid against a suspected murder? You'll have to excuse me——"

He broke off suddenly and looked sharply at Gruar.

"Wait a minute," he went on after a pause. "You're not asking me this for fun? I remember you talking about it on Saturday. Is there any connection?"

Gruar drew a line with his finger through the thin film of dust on the bonnet.

"There could be. Look, you're not going to enjoy what I'm going to say. I don't imagine you'll even believe it."

"Go on." Cattanach was serious now.

Gruar rubbed out the line with the back of his fist, and stood looking at the smear of dust across his knuckles.

"I'll start from my own end, and not from yours," he said. "That means starting from one assumption: this man died because there's a conference being held at Craggan. He died here, and he died now—because of that conference. I'd be a fool, and my lords and masters would call me one, if I didn't make that assumption."

"But I'm making the same assumption," Cattanach protested. "It's a case of murder——"

"Not quite the same. You see a body, you suspect murder, you look around for a suspect, because it's your job to get hold of murderers, and this is the first case of murder you've ever had to handle. I see a body, and what do I suspect? Espionage, first of all, and it's my job to stop that. So what do I want to know? Not who killed the man; but, who was he, how did he get near Craggan, whose plans were spoiled by his death, and how can I make something out of it? You get the point?"

"Yes. I don't like it much, but go on."

"Right. Now, you've got a suspect?"

"Yes. Macvartney."

"Why?"

"Not a very strong reason. But the murder happened when people from his old University turned up here, and there could have been a confusion of identity. This afternoon, too, I've unearthed a motive. Macvartney and Hakonson's wife have been lovers."

"Macvartney told you that?"

"Yes."

"He told me too. And some other things as well. He told me that Mrs. Wynrame and he saw a shadowy figure, as I believe the term goes, near Craggan lodge late on Friday night. He also told me that he saw Naverack handing over a lot of cash to an unknown man at Invermudale Hotel yesterday."

"Macvartney opens his mouth quite a lot."

"I'm not finished yet. There's a character with a revolver holed up some miles to the east of here in an old stable——"

"You mean Cornessie, don't you? Many's the time I've spent the night there in the old days."

"Yes. I'm told that's the name of the place. This man has been there since yesterday, and probably longer. He's being supplied with food from outside. Macvartney almost ran into him yesterday afternoon, just about the same time as I did. But Macvartney was a little earlier, and so he saw the man who supplies the food."

"Who?"

"Macvartney says it was Constable Thomson."

Cattanach's face went dangerously blank. He swung round on his heel towards his car.

"Sergeant Ross," he shouted. "Get that car reversed. We're going back to Corrachan."

"Wait a minute, wait a minute," said Gruar.

"I want to see Macvartney. He's got some explaining to do."

"You'd better listen to me first. I told you that you wouldn't enjoy it."

The car moved off slowly up the hill, making for a quarry three hundred yards ahead. Cattanach scuffed his foot in the dust.

"Hurry up, then. But I hope you aren't just going to repeat any more of Macvartney's stories."

"No. Some facts that seem to be relevant. Macvartney said that Thomson drove up the Invermudale road in a van with

"Winesack's Supermarkets" lettering on it, then walked over the hills to Cornessie. Now, I saw Thomson myself get into one of Winesack's vans at Rhintraid on Saturday. Also, Professor Naverack used to be Winesack's personal assistant, before he went to Perth University."

"Anything else?" Cattanach's foot was stationary now.

"Yes. Don't forget that Wynrame the keeper was carrying a rifle on Friday night. Again, I found some scraps of electric wire inside the conference room at Craggan on Saturday. They match the wire found in the dead man's pockets. I imagine it wasn't a coincidence that shortly after I left Craggan on Saturday Wynrame was busy up a tree that hangs pretty close to the house."

Sergeant Ross brought the car to a standstill. Cattanach signalled to him to switch the engine off. Baffled, Ross obeyed.

"And what do you think all this adds up to?" Cattanach was looking baffled himself.

"Enough to make me get our organisation busy. I've got some of the results here," Gruar said, taking his notebook from his pocket. "The most interesting is this: we've checked over Constable Thomson's record, as your office in Dalbreck gave it to me. It's a good record—in fact, completely clear, with one little exception. We've traced his relatives, schoolteachers, men who worked with him, and they all confirm what's on the record. There's no catch, and no question of mistaken identity."

"What's the exception?"

"Just this. Thomson told you that he was a merchant seaman before joining the police. What he didn't tell you was that he once spent two months between voyages in Murmansk. There was a row about it at the time. He missed his ship, and the Russians insisted that he wait until it came back to collect him on its next trip."

Cattanach's face had gone white. Gruar, taking his chance, went on quickly.

"One other thing. I put through a call to Glasgow police headquarters this morning—just to ask one question. The answer was rather interesting. When the deer poaching was at its peak, a year or two back, there was a good deal of evidence pointing at Winesack's organisation as the chief buyer and financier. Not enough to make a conviction possible, but enough for the police to be fairly certain about it."

"All right. Go on. Put it into plain words."

Gruar shoved his hands deep into his pockets and stared at the road.

"I don't know. But there seems to be some sort of link between Craggan and the poachers. Poaching isn't the paying game it was, yet McGlashan still comes to the strath. Is he running a courier service, or an escape route, as part of a spy system? I've told you before that we're worried about Dounreay. This may be one of the links in the chain. A little local help—Thomson, Wynrame, Macvartney, or someone else— and it would be easy to smuggle people in or out. Nobody is going to suspect poachers of being anything but poachers."

"So that's why you want me to keep an eye on McGlashan." Cattanach broke off and looked at his watch. "Almost six o'clock. I'll have to move if I'm going to locate him now."

"If you care to go to my office at Craggan," Gruar said mildly, "you can use the direct line to Dalbreck. I took the liberty, before I came after you, of alerting the police between here and Inverness. You ought to find a sheaf of reports waiting for you."

For an instant Cattanach was angry. Then he laughed.

"Sergeant Ross, turn that car again. I'm telling you, Mr. Gruar, it's going to be difficult to give my Chief Constable a proper explanation of all this. What do we do now?"

"If I've guessed right, there's some sort of ferrying job fixed for tonight—probably getting this man at Cornessie out. I don't know how valuable he is, so it may not matter if he gets away, but it is important that we find out who is involved in the strath, and just how the collection and delivery is managed. We may be able to roll up quite a long chain of agents that way. So I think we should arrange a little reception party for the poachers. I'd like them to get into the strath, pick up their load, and then be collected on the way out."

"And the reception party?"

Gruar smiled narrowly.

"The police ought to be represented, certainly—yourself and Constable Thomson. Sergeant Ross, when he's got his car turned, might be better employed down at Rhintraid, ready to chase the poachers on the main road. Then we'd better have a delegation from the deer forest owners, too. I think I can spare the time, and, if Mr. MacAra will let me, I'll bring a couple of keepers."

"And they will be——?"

"Wynrame and Macvartney. Oh yes, Wynrame and Macvartney seem to me eminently suited for this. I'll just go on to Corrachan and arrange that with Mr. MacAra."

CHAPTER EIGHT

GRUAR came out of Craggan, walking quickly, a sheaf of papers in his hand. He jumped in beside MacAra.

"Wynrame's house next, please," he said. "And then, if you'll drop us at the Halmidary hotel, you can get rid of us for good."

"Not before time," grumbled MacAra. A lifetime of keeping other people waiting had left him impatient himself. "Where's Inspector Cattanach?"

"Down at the hotel, seeing about a meal. It looks like business tonight, so we'll take the chance to eat now, for I don't know how long it may be till we get another."

Wynrame, it appeared, was out. Ann answered Gruar's knock. She didn't look towards the car. Alasdair, in the back seat, kept his own gaze rigidly forward. He could hear her cool voice, though he couldn't distinguish any words. If Gruar took much longer, he felt, he would know every leaf on the rhododendron bushes beside the road by heart. It seemed an age before Gruar got back into the car.

Round the first corner a guard was standing. Gruar lowered his window and spoke softly to him.

"Has Wynrame the keeper gone out in a car recently?"

"Yes, sir, about two hours ago. He went in the lodge shooting-brake."

"Right. Thank you."

MacAra drove on. Leaning back, Gruar passed a slip of paper to Alasdair.

"4.07 p.m. Relief party watching stable reports finding one agent dead, one unconscious with bullet wound: stable empty."

Gruar lit a cigarette and began to shuffle the papers in his hand.

"Wynrame was on the hill all morning; he came back just before four o'clock, and went out in the brake almost at once. You were at Corrachan all day, alone, until three o'clock."

"How do you know that?"

"I've just had a word with Mrs. Hakonson."

"When was your agent shot?"

"Sometime after one o'clock; the last routine wireless report came through then."

"That makes it nicely complicated for you, doesn't it?"

MacAra blew his horn violently at a startled sheep.

"It's all nothing to do with me " he said. "Are you making the salmon carry passes, Duncan?"

Something in the lawyer's tone made Gruar look up sharply.

"Do you think I like it all myself?" he retorted. "Next week this circus will be gone, and I'll be gone with them. But you'll still be here, both of you. I'd be glad to know where I'll be myself."

"Gently, gently," MacAra said. "I'm old and I could do with a drink. And I don't want anything to do with whatever you're up to. Just remember that."

They sat in silence until the car stopped outside the hotel. MacAra waited as they climbed out, nodded briefly, then drove on. They watched the car out of sight.

"He'd give twenty years to be handling this himself," Gruar said to Alasdair. "Come on. We've got to find Cattanach."

Cattanach was in Johnnie's office. There was a bottle on the table and a full glass. Gruar put the message from Craggan in front of him. The Inspector was about to speak when the telephone rang. He was across the room in a stride, knocking two chairs over in the process.

"Cattanach here," he said, engulfing the receiver in an enormous hand. "Is that you, Farquhar? Good. Any news? Where did you say? I see. All right."

He turned to Gruar.

"That confirms what we heard at Craggan," he said. "McGlashan has just been reported at Bonar Bridge. He's stopped at the hotel and gone in for a meal, so I reckon we've got about a couple of hours before he could come up the strath. It might be a lot later, of course."

Gruar looked at his watch.

"Half past six," he said. "What have you arranged?"

"I've sent Ross off with the patrol car," replied Cattanach. "He has been told to go to the Rhintraid police station and wait there until Constable McLeod gets up from Dalbreck on his motor bike. Then he's to send Thomson up here to meet us at eight o'clock. Ross and McLeod are to keep a watch for McGlashan at Rhintraid bridge. If they see him turn up the strath, they are to phone us at once, then get their car out and catch him at the bridge when he tries to run. Just to make certain, I've ordered your radio car to be ready to move from Dalbreck at a minute's notice."

"Good," said Gruar. "That seems to cover everything, more or less. I've ordered a Landrover fitted with radio to report here at half past seven, we've got hold of Alasdair here already, and that only leaves Wynrame. He went down the strath towards Rhintraid around four o'clock, and he's expected back soon. I told his wife that we would catch him as he comes through here. Alasdair, you'll sit at the hotel door and look out for Wynrame, or for a large black Chevrolet with three men in it. We'll go and eat. There should be plenty of time for you after we've finished."

So Alasdair ended up with a glass in his hand, watching the village settle down to its evening ritual—watching Mrs. Chisholm waddle across the road to call on Mrs. Macintagart, as she had done every evening except Sunday for the last thirty years, watching Lachie the shepherd from Kinloch trying hard not to stop at the bar on his way home; Lachie would be remembering that the last time his wife had given him a black eye that had taken weeks to wear off. It was all remote and inconsequent, a charade to be looked at from a distance. Once it had mattered a great deal that he had been on the outside, cut off from this closely-knit community. Now things were different. It was the first time he had been able to think quietly since he had met Erica Hakonson at Corrachan. Surprised, he was discovering that what he wanted was excitement, action. Violence, even the possibility of violence, was a far more powerful attraction than he had ever suspected. He tried not to think of Ann. Time enough for that later. Little as Gruar had told him, it was enough to let him realise that this trap for a poaching gang had something to do with the mystery hanging over Craggan. Solve that, and he could begin to think of Ann again —if she was still there to be thought about. And this time, he told himself, he would deal with the woman on his own terms.

After a while the fishermen began to come home. Alasdair took his glass and stood in the road outside, trying to look unobtrusive. Being there at all was a breach of protocol at that time of day. The proper place for him was the bar, where the ghillies were renewing their strength and reassuring each other of the extraordinary incompetence of their employers. It was a relief when Gruar and Cattanach came out and sent him inside to get his meal.

The dining-room was empty except for an elderly clergyman, who considerably startled Alasdair by asking him if he possessed a magnifying glass. On drawing a blank, the clergyman grunted and resumed a minute study of the local weekly newspaper. He was still immersed in this when Alasdair finished his meal twenty minutes later. In the hall outside he met Johnnie. In response to Alasdair's question, the hotel-keeper peered through the glass door of the dining-room and chuckled.

"Yon chap? He's an Irish Episcopalian dean or canon or archbishop or something. He's been spending the last two days with an advertisement in the paper. You see, it's advertising a bottle of whisky that he's never heard of before, and he can't quite make out the name of the distillery. He keeps pestering me about it. Maybe I'll tell him where to get the stuff before he leaves, but, ach, the fellow is always telling me that Irish whiskey is better than Scotch, so he can be waiting a bit longer before he tastes this one."

Outside, Gruar and Cattanach were walking up and down, pursued by the first of the evening midges. Cattanach was an attractive target, clearly, and was resenting it.

"The brutes are bad the night," was his first remark as Alasdair came up to them. "We'd be safer in the hotel." He led the retreat himself, Gruar and Alasdair following.

"We've seen Wynrame," Gruar said. "He's gone off home for a meal, and he'll be back by eight." He flicked a persistent midge out of his hair. "I hope these damned things settle down a bit later. What we need is a cold snap to knock them off."

A cold snap was the last thing to be expected from the weather. The rain of Friday night had been an isolated storm. Now the sky was clear again, the wind soft from the south-east, the river dropping rapidly from want of rain. As so often in the Highlands, the best of the summer weather was coming at its very beginning. It was odds on that August would be a wet and cold catastrophe by comparison.

Came eight o'clock, and punctual to the minute Thomson's green car drove up the road from Rhintraid. A few minutes later Wynrame's brake drew in alongside the radio Landrover from Craggan. Wynrame got out, and walked away round the back of the hotel. When he reappeared after five minutes the remainder of the party were grouped around the Landrover, laying down a protective barrage of tobacco smoke against the midges.

Cattanach was speaking.

"You've all been warned why we're here. It looks as if that man McGlashan and his gang may be coming up the strath tonight. Don't get the idea that this is a special occasion, just because I've turned out myself. I've probably spent more nights out after poachers than all the rest of you put together, but today I'm going to take advice from those who've been at the game recently. That means you, Thomson, and you, Wynrame."

"Very good, sir," said Thomson. Wynrame nodded without speaking. He was shuttered and barred again, anonymous and aloof, the perfect butler masquerading as a gamekeeper. And he was Ann's husband; the stab of jealousy startled Alasdair, made him realise that he couldn't keep her out of his mind as easily as he had imagined.

"Well, then, what do you two reckon the poachers will do?" Cattanach asked. "Sergeant Ross is at Rhintraid, and he'll telephone us as soon as they turn up the strath. Do you think they'll come early or late?"

"Late would be sensible," Wynrame said. "The deer will be nearer the road by dusk, and the car won't be so easily spotted. They came late when they killed those hinds near Kinloch last week."

"You don't think they would pull a bluff, and come straight up early in the evening, reckoning that we wouldn't be expecting them then?" Gruar asked.

Thomson shook his head, before Wynrame could speak.

"I doubt it. Too many other cars about. Anyway, Sergeant Ross is going to warn us."

Cattanach looked quickly at Wynrame, then at Alasdair, saw the agreement in their faces, and nodded.

"We'll have to wait for Ross, anyway," he said, "but I don't think he'll be calling for a while yet."

Alasdair looked at his watch. 8.20. He lit a cigarette and wandered across the road to the steps of the hall. He squatted there, out of the direct sunlight, and watched the midges close in on Cattanach. It wasn't very long, however, before he was under fire himself. After ten minutes he had had as much as he could stand. He got up and began to pace the road.

The village was quiet. A stray ewe with her lamb moved slowly along the ditch beside the road, a crow called out of the fir plantation. Twenty paces up, twenty paces back, and all the time in front of the five pairs of eyes by the Landrover. 8.30. 8.45. He felt himself pacing more rapidly, checked it, and went off on a circuit round the hotel.

He was half-way round when he noticed the telephone cable. It had been neatly sliced with a knife. He was climbing over an empty beer-crate to look more closely when Cattanach came round the corner.

The Inspector saw the cable before Alasdair had time to speak. He gave Alasdair a long, hard look, then swung round on his heel. Alasdair followed more slowly.

When he reached the Landrover Cattanach was already speaking.

"Somebody"—he emphasised the word heavily—"has cut the hotel telephone cable, so Sergeant Ross may have been trying to get in touch with us already."

"Wouldn't he ring the post office if he couldn't get the hotel?" suggested Gruar. "I'll go and find out."

When he came back his face was serious.

"There's some sort of a break between here and Rhintraid," he reported. "Halmidary isn't a busy exchange, and nobody's tried to put a call through in the last hour, so this is the first the operator's known of it."

"I see," said Cattanach slowly. "Now where are we? Has this anything to do with the poachers, do you think?"

Nobody spoke. The Inspector glanced from face to face before speaking again.

"Since the Sergeant can't get in touch with us, there's a chance that McGlashan is in the strath already. We'd better go down and have a look for him."

Alasdair was surprised. It wasn't so long since they had all agreed that the poachers were likely to come late rather than early. Now Cattanach was wanting to run the risk of bungling the whole carefully prepared operation. By going down now, they were liable to find McGlashan too soon, before he had begun his actual poaching operations, or even to arrive at Rhintraid before he entered the strath.

Wynrame thought as much, evidently, for he protested.

"I wouldn't call that very sensible, Inspector," the keeper said. "Would it not be better to wait a bit, or to send Constable Thomson here down to find out what's happened?"

Gruar cut in quickly.

"I think the Inspector's right. My guess is that these wires haven't been cut for fun. If I'm right, the sooner we move the better."

Thomson opened his mouth to speak, then thought better of it, for Cattanach had begun to move already.

"We'll need two cars," said Gruar. "I can take two people

in the Landrover. Wynrame, could you drive your own car, and bring the Inspector with you? Thomson, Macvartney, with me."

Gruar threw the Landrover round in a close turn, tyres squealing. Then they were off down the Rhintraid road. Alasdair, sandwiched between Gruar and Thomson, said little. Through the driving-mirror he could see Wynrame's brake trailing well behind.

Two miles out, on the top of a rise, Gruar slowed down. He reached across and pulled a pair of binoculars from the dashboard locker.

"Use these," he said to Alasdair. "And watch the road ahead."

Down past Kinloch, through a depressed clump of fir trees, and out on a bare shoulder of hill. The river was swinging away to the west in a broad loop. At the top of the hill Gruar stopped to allow a black car come slowly up and pass them. For a moment Alasdair thought that they had failed, that this was McGlashan, about to drive through them towards Invermudale and safety. Then he realised that the car was far too small. As it came nearer its driver was revealed as a bearded gentleman in a turban.

"Get on with it," Gruar said to Alasdair. "You've got a job to do."

Guiltily, Alasdair put the binoculars to his eyes.

Beyond the shoulder the road and river came together again. This was the last real chance, and the best one, for the flats by the water were a favourite place for the deer, which rarely came down any nearer to Rhintraid. There, too, a poacher was far from any houses, and out of ear-shot of the nearest keeper at Kinloch. Along the roadside, birch woods gave a good deal of cover, enough to hide a car from long-range observation. If a poacher wanted to snatch a few beasts before dusk, this was his best chance in the whole strath.

Alasdair took his time with the binoculars. With the evening coming on, the wind was dropping. In the stillness the sound of the river came and went. As he watched, a heron came up the valley, its long wings flapping ponderously at the air. A wood pigeon rose from the trees along the road. Its call came huskily across the heather, followed by an answering chorus, as a dozen more broke out of the birches and hustled indignantly away downstream. Alasdair stiffened, and swung the glasses towards the trees. Something had disturbed the birds. A hunting buzzard? But there was no hovering speck in the clear sky. A fox, a weasel, even a wild-cat? Perhaps. But there was another possibility.

Gruar nodded when Alasdair told him. Behind, Wynrame drew up.

"There may be something there. We'll go down pretty fast and drive to the far edge of the wood, then stop and have a look. Constable, tell the Inspector what's happening."

Thomson ran back, gave his message and jumped into the Landrover as it pulled out of the passing place. Gruar was accelerating hard, throwing the machine round a succession of sharp curves at a pace that left Wynrame far behind. The birches came up to engulf them, cutting out the sunlight and dappling the road with a shower of molten emeralds. Gruar braked as they swooped over a little stone bridge, then rushed away up a slope. They came to the crest, swept round to the right, and saw the glint of sunlight at the end of the tunnel of trees.

So sharp was the light that for an instant neither Alasdair nor Gruar saw the car. When they did, it was almost too late. It was standing in the middle of the road, in a dip that half cut it off from sight, leaving only the upper bodywork showing. Gruar shoved his foot down hard, swearing as he did so. The tyres squealed, the car swayed and slid, the smell of burning rubber hit Alasdair's nostrils—but they stopped with two yards to spare.

What happened then was too quick for Alasdair to take in. There was a man, he remembered afterwards, standing in the road with a gun. Beyond, at the car door, there was another. For an instant his reflexes refused to act, and in that time Thomson was out of the car, running towards the man with the gun. There was a shout, a shot that sent pellets pattering through the birches, a scuffle and then Thomson staggered and fell. Alasdair ran past him down the road, gaining fast on the gunman as he sprinted away. The black car's engine roared; a door opened; first one man and then the other jumped in. For an instant Alasdair still gained; he put one hand on the car. Then it was gone, and he was left in the middle of the track, smelling the acrid blue smoke that curled slowly in the evening air.

Gruar came to his elbow, panting. Together they watched the black car sweep out of the birch tunnel and into the sunlight. Behind there was the sound of brakes and the slamming of doors. It had taken so little time that Wynrame had only caught up with them after everything was over.

They went back to where Wynrame and Cattanach were helping Thomson to his feet. The policeman was holding his stomach and gasping, but showed no other signs of injury.

"What happened?" Cattanach asked.

Gruar told him.

"So we guessed right," was the Inspector's comment. "Would you be able to identify the men, do you think?"

"I expect so," said Gruar.

"Well, now we've got something to go on. Assaulting the police, discharging a firearm recklessly, perhaps a poaching conviction if we're lucky. Ross should be able to stop them at Rhintraid bridge."

"They seemed a bit violent," said Gruar. "Will he manage with only two men against three?"

"I don't think they'd risk any nonsense so near the village," said Cattanach. "Too public, for one thing. But we'll get down there and see what's happened. Ross has his orders to stop that car."

"How are you now, Thomson?" asked Gruar.

"Winded, that's all, sir, I think. But I'm not up to much just yet."

"A pity," Cattanach said. "Still, we'll have to get on. Ready, Gruar?"

Wynrame cut in.

"If you like, sir, I could bring Constable Thomson in my car and let the rest of you go on in front. You might make better speed without him."

"That's sensible. All right. Wait at the bridge. We'll see you there, unless we have to go on further after the poachers."

They started off again, leaving Thomson sitting on the grass beside Wynrame's brake. The bridge was slow in coming, for all Gruar's speed. Once they met a tourist head-on and had to reverse. Once they skidded viciously on a corner and sank a rear wheel into soft peat-bog at the road's edge. Cattanach was angry and worried. He asked one question only, but it was enough to show he had made his mind up.

"Was it a genuine fight, do you think, Macvartney?"

"I just couldn't say, sir. The shot was harmless, for the gun was pointing in the other direction, and the blow could have been a fake for all that I could see."

"Anyway, we've got something to go on now. I hope Ross has done his job."

But Ross hadn't. When they pulled to a halt at Rhintraid bridge, half a mile above the village, he was standing in the road, dusty and disconsolate, Constable McLeod with him.

Cattanach was out in a flash.

"What's happened to you? Where's the black car? Did he slip you? Where's your car? Why aren't you chasing him?" Excitement was having its usual effect on the Inspector's speech.

Ross was flustered and apologetic. Yes, they had left the car at the police station and gone on foot to watch the strath road. They had seen the car turn up the strath. But when they went to the police station they couldn't get a phone call through to Halmidary. Then their car wouldn't start, and Constable McLeod's cycle wouldn't either, and the only garageman in Rhintraid was away on a hire to Inverness with the only hiring car. And Mr. MacAra wasn't in, and before they could try to get another car from Dalbreck, the black car came down again. Ross had tried to stop it by waving, but had had to jump to safety when it didn't stop. And that was just seven minutes before.

Cattanach looked at his watch indecisively. He obviously wanted to have a row. A cut telephone wire, a damaged car; and now the poachers getting away again, after putting themselves within his grasp. But it wasn't Sergeant Ross's fault—at least, not sufficiently to allow Cattanach to turn on him in public. And as a result he didn't know where to begin.

Gruar was busy with the controls of the radio in the back of the Landrover. He raised his hand for silence as he flicked a switch. After listening for a few seconds, he picked up the hand microphone and spoke. Meanwhile Cattanach, black anger in his face, prowled restlessly up and down.

"That's done," said Gruar, climbing down on to the road. "The radio car is waiting to pick these characters up just outside Dalbreck. Now we must hurry. Sergeant, take this machine and get after them."

"Good," said Cattanach. "I'd better go too."

"I'd prefer you to stay with us, Inspector," Gruar said quickly. "There you are, Sergeant, off you go."

It was done with decision. Ross and McLeod got into the Landrover and started off, Cattanach shouting instructions about the charges to be made against the men when they were caught. Gruar called him back urgently.

"Come on now. Off the road before anyone comes along."

Cattanach and Alasdair followed him obediently as he vaulted over a fence and ducked under the shoreward arch of the bridge.

"Just in time," he said.

A car was coming down the strath. It drew nearer, then stopped on the bridge, right over their heads. A door banged, and there was the sound of voices.

"They've gone on, by the look of it." The voice was Wynrame's.

"That was a near thing," Thomson replied. "We made a mess of it by both dealing with the telephone, and I'm not sure that the fight didn't look phoney. Do you think McGlashan will get away?"

Cattanach drew his breath in sharply. This was decisive, now; he was hearing with his own ears proof of Thomson's complicity.

"I don't know," Wynrame said. "Someone seems to have rumbled this poaching stunt, so Igor's safer where he is tonight. We'd better check if the police car is still at your house."

"It will be. They won't get that to go again in five minutes."

Cattanach waved a silent and savage fist in the air.

"We'll make sure, all the same," Wynrame said. "You'll have work to do tonight, and that car could be a nuisance if they got it started. I'm going back to pick up Igor and get him under cover again. He'll go out tomorrow night."

"Which means——" Thomson left his sentence unfinished.

"Which means just what you think. The McGlashan route is closed now. And we're all getting out."

"Channel Z," Thomson said eagerly.

"Yes. Channel Z. You've got to operate it tonight. I want to take my load out tomorrow, and now Igor will have to come too. So you'd better start moving. Make for Grangemouth once you've passed on the message. Come on."

CHAPTER NINE

THE car door slammed, the engine started, and the two men were gone. The three under the bridge waited a few minutes, then climbed out. Gruar cocked an eye at Cattanach, who grunted his anger in reply.

"Yes. You've got something here, Mr. Gruar. But what are we to do about it?"

Gruar started to walk across the bridge and down the half mile of road that separated them from the village proper.

"There's not very much time to spare," he said. "Wynrame will be coming back pretty soon, and we've got to be off this road before he does."

"Where are we going?" panted Cattanach, settling into a stride beside the others.

"We can forget about Wynrame. He won't move until to-morrow. The important thing is to follow Thomson and try to see just how he works Channel Z. So you and I are going to watch Thomson's house, and Alasdair is going to break into Mr. MacAra's garage and get his car out," said Gruar. As he walked he pulled out the inevitable pad from his pocket, stopped briefly to scribble a note on it, and handed the piece of paper to Alasdair.

"There you are. If MacAra's in his house show him that. If not, get into the garage somehow. If the car's gone, then find one somewhere else. And be back inside twenty minutes whatever you do."

"Where shall I come?" Alasdair asked.

"Don't leave the main street," said Gruar. "We don't want to show the car near Thomson's house. Wait at the post office. I don't imagine it will be very long before things happen."

Alasdair looked at his watch. It was only ten o'clock. So much had happened in the last hour that time had ceased to have much meaning.

Now they were approaching the first houses of the village. Gruar and Cattanach left the road and took a narrow footpath running away up the hill from the river. That way, Alasdair knew, they would emerge behind the row of council houses where the police station and Thomson's house stood. He put on speed, acutely conscious of the emptiness of the road in the twilight, and expecting every minute to see Wynrame's car appear and catch him without any chance of taking cover. There was also the thought of an interview with MacAra ahead.

The houses on either side thickened into a street. Shops began to appear, the post office, a bar. Fifty yards ahead he saw the opening that led to the harbour and MacAra's office. The lawyer's house lay a hundred yards further on. A car's horn sounded behind him. He stopped and turned to look, standing close to the wall of a house. Wynrame's brake came slowly on to the street, and turned away from Alasdair, heading back towards the bridge and the strath.

MacAra was opening the front door of his house when Alasdair reached it. He had been drinking, but the signs were hard to see. His walk was steady, there was no fumbling as he felt for the lock with his key—but he had been drinking, probably hard enough to have put most men under the table.

Alasdair showed him the note without speaking, and waited. MacAra read it through twice, then nodded.

"Right you are. Take the thing."

He threw a bunch of keys to Alasdair, pushed the front door open and took a step inside. Then he turned slowly.

"Tell me—does that man Gruar think he's nearly finished all this business?"

"I don't know at all, Mr. MacAra. I don't know what the business is, come to that."

MacAra was sombre, judicial, a whisky-fortified Calvin.

"I'll tell you then. He isn't a factor or a lawyer, and he knows a lot less about salmon than you or I. But he's not a policeman, though he's chasing these poachers, and he knows a damned sight more than Cattanach does about what's going on in this sinful strath. There's something odd happening at Craggan Lodge, and he knows all about it. What do *you* know?"

Unpredictable in the grip of the whisky, MacAra was looking for comfort now. He had stopped short of saying what he knew himself; some last flicker of caution was burning up. But the man felt lost, out of the picture, and he resented it. Alasdair tried to be pacific.

"I like Mr. Gruar fine, Mr. MacAra. Right now he's on the track of these poachers, and I don't want to keep him waiting. I'll just go and get the car out, if I may."

"Off you go, then." Now MacAra was curt, dismissive. Alasdair took his chance and went. He was just turning the corner of the house to go to the garage when the lawyer called after him.

"How are you getting on with the woman, Alasdair?" This was the MacAra he had heard about, the MacAra of younger days, an expert showing an expert's interest in a subject he knew well. In the voice Alasdair could trace excitement, envy. Small wonder that there were a lot of men who still had scores to remember against the old kelt. But Alasdair's own reaction was immediate.

"What are you talking about, Mr. MacAra?" The tone was as frigid as he dared make it, but MacAra was too far gone to notice.

"You know fine. And I know, and Gruar knows, and Wattie knows, and half the strath has its own ideas. But never mind. It'll do Wynrame no harm, the sour old devil, if you get hold of her. Good luck to it." He laughed harshly, hesitated a second, and then slammed the door.

Alasdair opened the garage, and took out the shooting brake. So it was as clear as that. And he had thought that he was keeping control pretty well. A slow unreasoning anger burned up inside him. Damn them all; damn MacAra for kicking him in the teeth; damn Gruar, always the mystery man, suspecting and plotting and pushing him into impossible situations; damn

Thomson and Wynrame and the poachers and the whole lot of them. Damn himself, for getting into this mess.

He was in the same mood when he brought the car to a halt outside the post office. It was darkening fast; the sun was down and a cold breeze from the North Sea was beginning to rustle along the street. A fish lorry rumbled past him, piled high with boxes and dripping a trail of water. Its tail lights receded away southwards, red eyes of a timid dragon retreating into its lair. A motor cycle followed it, the rider black against the horizon as he disappeared round the seaward end of the street. Then silence; the street was empty, and his thoughts took full command.

It was only for five minutes. Running feet sounded, coming down a side turning and out into the road, coming his way. He switched on the engine, and moved slowly forward.

His guess was right. It was Gruar and behind him, a grampus after a shark, Cattanach. He slowed down, and Gruar pulled the door open.

"Turn round, Alasdair, and get after that motor bike. Thomson's on it."

The two men jumped in. Alasdair threw the car into the nearest opening, reversed crazily into the main road, and pulled away in pursuit of the cycle. Behind his head he could hear Cattanach panting. Then the road claimed all his attention.

The shooting brake was old and heavy and perverse. Holding it on course was difficult, getting speed out of it was a conjuring trick. Somehow he managed to keep the cumbersome brute under control; somehow the miles began to slide past. But the bike had five minutes start, and there was the fish lorry to be remembered. The road was twisty, if double-tracked, and passing was going to be difficult, with every second counting.

They came up to the lorry at a sharp double corner, where the road cut a horseshoe course into the hillside to cross a stream. For an agonising age Alasdair had to crawl in low gear round the bends, losing all the momentum he had painfully built up, not daring to risk passing. Then they were out on to a straight, up the face of the open hillside, and he could

I

see again. The brake was slow to accelerate; they crept past the lorry inch by inch, the smell of the fish flooding in through the open windows, Alasdair praying all the time that nothing would come down the hill in the opposite direction. But nothing did come, and they swept over the crest into the darkness of the further side. He relaxed in his seat for the first time since they had left Rhintraid.

Gruar was relaxing too.

"Good work, Alasdair. But we'll have to hurry. Thomson has got Constable McLeod's motor cycle. He must have hidden some parts, and then replaced them when he wanted to use it himself. He's on serious business tonight all right. I'd like to know just what Channel Z is, and he'll lead us to it if we're quick enough."

They were in Dalbreck now. Cattanach leaned forward and pointed.

"See there. That's the poachers' car outside the police office. Looks as if the radio car got them."

The radio car was standing outside the office also, and the Landrover too. As far as catching the poachers went, the operation had been successful. But where was Thomson?

Alasdair pulled up behind the poachers' saloon. All three jumped out. Cattanach ran to the office door and shouted inside. Almost instantly four uniformed officers came out, Ross and McLeod amongst them.

"What's happened, Ross?" Cattanach asked.

"The other car got the poachers just outside the town, sir," replied the Sergeant. "We're just going to charge them now."

"Don't worry about that. Hold them for a bit until things are quieter. Has anyone here seen a motor cycle go through in the last ten minutes?"

"Yes, sir," said McLeod. "I saw one from the office window. It went south."

"It was your own machine," said Cattanach. "We'll have to get after it. Where's the radio car driver? Get him out here at once."

The driver was found and pushed into his car in two minutes

flat, Cattanach fuming at every second's delay. Alasdair and Gruar climbed in also. Then they were off, Cattanach and another man in plain clothes scrambling aboard as they started.

"Hurry," was the Inspector's only instruction. "Straight on the south road."

The driver hurried. However fast the motor cycle might be, they must be gaining on it now. If only Thomson hadn't slipped off the road somewhere. If that had happened, then the whole chase was pointless, and Channel Z was safe from them. The next half hour would show. Alasdair leaned back and closed his eyes.

But Gruar had business on his mind. As the big car exploded along the coast road in the half-dark of the northern night, he was speaking quietly to the second man in the front of the car. There came the sound of switches, then dials glowed on the passenger's side of the dashboard.

Gruar leaned over, picked up a microphone and talked into it.

"Black to red. Come in now. Over."

A loudspeaker crackled metallically.

"Red to black. Receiving you. Over."

"Black to red. Report. Over."

"Red to black. Keeper Wynrame returned home ten minutes ago. No other movement since eight o'clock. Over."

"Black to red. Put on emergency patrols at once. Keep Craggan grounds clear until I get in touch again. Over."

"Red to black. Understood. Off."

Gruar sat back.

"That's that," he said. "Now where are we getting to?"

It wasn't very clear. They were a dozen miles from Dalbreck already, still going fast. Ahead the coast-line was broken by an estuary, across which a suspension bridge carried the road high above the water. On the far bank the railway rejoined the road, after a wide detour inland over the Shellachan pass. A passenger train was rushing down the line, its coaches brightly lit against the dark hillside.

"The 9.25 at Halmidary," Cattanach said. "It won't be into Inverness till almost midnight."

Alasdair was jolted into attention. Did Channel Z run through Inverness? He put his thoughts into words, and Gruar nodded.

"Could be. Or anywhere along the way. We'll have to check the stations as we go."

The driver called back from the front seat.

"There's a light on the road ahead of us, sir. It's just turned on to the bridge."

"Keep him in sight, driver," said Gruar, "but don't get too close. I want to see if he gets on to the train."

They closed in on the retreating streak of light ahead—over the suspension bridge, along a straight, up to a humped bridge over the railway. As they crossed the bridge the train roared and rumbled beneath them. Beyond the road turned left, between houses with ground floors in darkness. A filling station, deserted for the night, a war memorial, glistening in the beam from their headlights, and then a long, empty straight.

"Stop where you can't be seen from the station," ordered Gruar.

The driver pulled up hard. A whistle sounded, an answering peep came from the engine, hissing in frustration, and then the train was pulling on its way south. Gruar got out, Cattanach with him, and ran into the station yard. They were back inside a minute, grinning.

"Got him," said Cattanach. "He's on the train, and that's McLeod's cycle he's left here. If we can't do anything else, at least we'll be able to nail him for malicious damage and theft. I'll have him out of the force before I've finished."

Gruar was grave. "There's a good deal more serious business than that involved. We've got to get on to that train and see what Thomson's up to. He may not wait until Inverness. What's the best thing to do, Inspector? You know the country better than I do. Where could we get aboard without being spotted?"

This was a problem Cattanach could understand. He answered at once.

"If we go to Grudie Station we can get the station master to slip us in on the wrong side of the train. It's a single platform station on a curve, and we can get into the guard's van without much chance of being seen. But we'll have to hurry to get there ahead of the train. Get started, driver."

They went even faster than before. Grudie was three stations away down the line, and the road was a winding one, with few straights to allow high speeds. The train was also in a hurry, and its stops were brief. At the first station it was still ahead by seconds. Gruar looked anxious. The longer Thomson was alone the more chance that he would be able to pass on his message. But then the road improved slightly, and the car pulled ahead. They were well past the second station before Alasdair spotted the train approaching it, and when they roared into Grudie it was nowhere in sight.

"You come too, Jim," snapped Gruar to the operator. "He doesn't know you by sight and you may come in useful. Driver, can you work the transmitter?"

"Yes, sir."

"Good. Call up Craggan when we've gone and tell them what's happened. And telephone the Inverness railway police and ask them to have someone ready to meet us."

Then they were on the platform, listening. Cattanach was in the station office, talking urgently to the startled station master and showing his identification papers. A whistle sounded in the distance; time was getting short. The station master came running out, and waved them to follow him. He went to the back of the platform, and motioned them to cross the line and stand opposite him.

"You'll be about right there. But keep well clear till she stops."

Another whistle, and the clatter of wheels crossing a bridge. Alasdair drew back up the bank far enough, he hoped, to be clear of the light from the carriage windows. Then the train was on them, thundering, slowing reluctantly, grinding sparks as it came to a halt. There was the noise of a bolt being drawn, and above their heads the door of the guard's van opened. A voice called.

"Quick, now."

They climbed up an unexpected dark wall of metal and wood and pulled themselves into the van on their hands and knees. Cattanach swore softly and rubbed his knuckles. A voice called "Right away", a whistle sounded, and the engine gave a gargantuan snort of triumph. The guard swung lightly into the van and pulled his door shut behind him. They were aboard.

The guard looked curiously at the four as they stood up and shook themselves tidy.

"Man, the police are up to an awful lot nowadays, but I'm seeing that they still need the trains to help them in the end." He laid down his lantern and pulled a key out of his pocket.

"Here, I'll let you travel first class in honour of the occasion. It's not often I get an Inspector of Police wanting a lift in my van."

Gruar stopped him.

"I think we'll get someone to take a look through the train before we get into a carriage. It wouldn't do to be seen."

The guard looked solemn.

"So you're after someone on the train. Is he one of these desperate men I'm always seeing on the television nowadays?"

"Maybe. But you let this man here"—Gruar gestured to Jim —"go and have a prowl along the train before you push us all out of here."

Gruar turned to Jim.

"Have you seen Thomson before?"

"No, sir."

"All the better. He won't know you either."

Gruar described Thomson briefly, and Jim went off down the corridor. He was away ten minutes, and came back as the train slowed at another station.

"He's there, sir, two carriages away, in plain clothes."

"Right. Now get out with the guard and make sure he doesn't leave the train here."

The same procedure was repeated at each station. Alasdair relaxed in the plush splendours of a first-class carriage and counted the minutes until they would reach Inverness. As time went on it looked more and more likely that Thomson was going all the way. The guard was sent off to investigate, and came back to report that he had a single ticket to Inverness. Cattanach chewed uneasily at the events of the night, planning what he would do to a member of his force who behaved in such a way.

"How did you get on to Thomson?" he asked Gruar.

"Luck—and a coincidence. It was seeing him go into Winesack's van on Saturday morning that set me thinking, for I'd heard rumours about Winesack being tied up with deer poaching. After that it began to fall into place. The poachers were in the strath on Thursday night, Thomson was up at Craggan on Friday night—and then the dead man appeared. When Alasdair here spotted him coming back from Cornessie on Sunday afternoon the whole thing made sense."

The train rolled across the Beauly river as Cattanach digested the information.

"So the poaching is tied up with spying, and Thomson is a spy?" he said half to himself. "That doesn't help me to solve my problem."

"Perhaps not. But it does tell you how the dead man got here. That's how the mysterious Igor came, too. And it may be worth remembering that Professor Naverack is a friend of Winesack's too."

Alasdair sat upright with a start. This was something that hadn't hit him. But before he could speak Jim pushed the compartment door open.

"Thomson's beginning to pack up," he reported.

Gruar stood up.

"We'd better get ready too. I expect it'll be the usual business of meeting a contact on the platform. These people tend to use the same tricks over and over again."

They got out of the compartment and moved one carriage nearer their quarry, Jim leading and Alasdair last. Alasdair was worried. Something was nagging at the back of his mind. It all seemed too easy. What if Thomson was going to pass the message before he reached the station? But how could he? There were no more stops before Inverness, and the train was moving smartly. Alasdair reviewed what would happen when they arrived. He knew what the train would do. It would slow down to creep through the swing bridge at the entrance to the Caledonian Canal, then accelerate on to the high bridge across the River Ness. If he looked out as they crossed the river, he would be able to see the lights of the station to his right. But the train would swing away from the lights, and sweep on into the blackness on his left hand. For Inverness was not like other stations. In shape it resembled a triangle, with the station offices at the apex and the platforms forming the two sides. One set of platforms pointed north, towards Dingwall and the lines to Kyle of Lochalsh and Caithness; the others faced south-east, and the trains left them for Aberdeen or the long haul across the Grampians to Perth. The base of the triangle had no platforms, but simply formed a through link between the two main lines. To the confusion of strangers, incoming trains did not run straight in to their respective platforms, but instead went across the base of the triangle, and then reversed into the opposite side. This made for ease of traffic handling, for passengers from the north could simply walk across into another train for the south, instead of working their way up one side of the triangle and down the other. But it was going to mean trouble, Alasdair thought. A halt in the dark, whilst the signals changed, would be a perfect opportunity for Thomson to jump from the train, or to pass a message to someone waiting. And at the station he might be able to get away through the shunting lines and sheds.

But there was something else, something they had all overlooked. Alasdair groped for it, uneasily aware that time was running out.

"He's gone into the lavatory," Jim whispered from the corner of his mouth as he moved back across the join of the two carriages from the coach in which Thomson was travelling. To confirm his words came the slam of a door and sound of a bolt being slid home. Gruar raised his eyebrows.

"We'll search that one too," he murmured.

Thomson came out and went into his own compartment, leaving the door open behind him. The train began to lose speed.

"Inverness already," Cattanach said.

But it wasn't. Alasdair suddenly realised what was happening. They were slowing for the canal bridge, slowing almost to a halt. And then it dawned on him. His first thought was that he was too late, that Thomson would get away with it. For he knew now how Channel Z worked.

"Quick, open the windows and watch the canal," he shouted. But they were standing close behind each other, and it was difficult to move. Alasdair ran back to the first door he could find and pulled the window down. The train was on the bridge. Thomson was leaning out of a window, a torch in his hand flashing urgently. There was an answering flash down beside the water. Then the train was pulling away. And at last a door opened ahead of him, as he wrestled with the handle of his own one.

It was Jim who jumped, rolling over and over down the bank as he did so. He was up almost at once, and running towards the water. A flash of flame, small and thin against the pillar of fire from the engine, a sharp angry crack, and Jim toppled over and lay still. At last Alasdair had his own door open and was beginning to swing himself out, when Gruar's hand fell on his shoulder and pulled him back.

"Too late, we're going too fast now. And there's Thomson up ahead of us with a gun, and God knows what down by the water there. You'll be more use when we get into the station."

"Pull the communication cord, blast you," said Alasdair, "that man may be dying out there."

"It wouldn't do any good. It'll be quicker to wait till we get to the station now. Cattanach, let me past you to that door. I've got a gun and I think we're going to need it."

Thomson must know now that he's been trailed, must know

that there are people on the train who want to get him, thought Alasdair. But he's operated Channel Z. Perhaps it's been worth it, perhaps nothing else matters to him. The morbid curiosity to pry into the mind of a desperate man, a man almost certainly doomed, standing there in the quietness of a deserted, dingy train compartment, took violent hold of Alasdair. It was as if he had nothing to do with what was happening, but was a detached and pitiless observer from another dimension.

The lights of the platform loomed up to their right and then disappeared as the train rushed unheeding into the blackness of the shunting yards. Gruar looked cautiously out.

"I can still see his shadow outside the window," he reported. "He hasn't moved. Alasdair, get to the door on the other side of the coach and be ready to tell me if he doubles back. Cattanach, you follow me, but look out. When you're clear, get the railway police."

Thomson had one last advantage. His coach was old, and each compartment had a separate door, with another directly opposite across the corridor. But the first class coach in which the others were travelling was a grander affair. There was no way to get out of the compartments except into the corridor, and there were doors only at each end of the coach. As a result, they could not hope to move out all together and swamp the fugitive by numbers. He could keep them guessing until the very last second.

The train stopped. Gruar watched and listened. Still Thomson stood motionless, his shadow sharp and clear in the warm yellow rectangle of light from the window. The engine groaned, and then slowly began to move backwards, pushing its coaches towards the southbound platform. Now, surely now, Thomson must do something.

He did. The platform glided into sight in the corner of Alasdair's eye, as he watched the dark lines of the engine-shed and goods station on his side of the track. There was the sound of a carriage door being opened. Gruar threw his own open and jumped, gun in hand, shouting almost before he landed.

"The other side, Alasdair, the other side. Watch for him."

There was a rush of movement in the corridor ahead, another door was torn open, and then Alasdair was jumping, stumbling, half-falling, and picking himself up to cannon into a running figure. A shot, a tear at his sleeve, and Thomson was past him, dodging his way across the sleepers. Alasdair lunged, felt a shoulder slide through his grasp, caught a leg and clung to an ankle, was dragged by the sheer momentum of the man's rush, and then let go in agony as his wrist was cracked against a rail. But Thomson was falling too, tripping over the rail, and lurching on to the next track—and then he was screaming in terror. Alasdair was aware of an immense mass of darkness with a gleaming eye in its midst, the shriek of metal on metal, and a low, horrible bump. Then he was staring in silence at a huge driving wheel, and the crushed remains of a revolver.

*　　*　　*

In the thin, cold light of early morning Gruar came into the hotel room and sat down heavily. He took a revolver out of his pocket, emptied the chambers and put the gun away again. Alasdair poured out a cup of black coffee from the tray in front of him and pushed it over. Gruar took it without speaking, drank a mouthful and then lit a cigarette.

"I wasn't very clever about that. I was fooled by the door. He must have thrown it open and then slipped back in as soon as he saw me jumping. I never was much good at this side of the business really, and I'd better leave it to other people."

"He died at once, didn't he?" asked Alasdair. The question was pointless. Nothing else could have happened.

"Yes. Cattanach is getting the record straight with the railway police and the local superintendent now. I'd rather be out of that."

"When did Thomson go wrong?"

"In Murmansk, I imagine, though we'll probably never know. At any rate, he must have come back to Britain with a definite plan to get himself worked into the police. Cattanach says he volunteered to leave a desk job at Dalbreck to fill the vacancy at Rhintraid—which makes it look as if he was always marked out as a link man for whatever's been going on at Craggan. They take a lot of trouble, these Russians, for even a small sideline."

"And Channel Z?"

"He opened it, I'm pretty certain. When we got round to the canal bank we found Jim unconscious with a broken arm. He's in no danger. There was no trace of the man who collected the message, and a radio-equipped boat is missing from the harbour tonight. The town police are on to that now, and they may find something—that is, if the boat does come back and isn't simply scuttled. But we'd better take it that Channel Z has worked this time. It won't again."

"So what?" Alasdair was tired, desperately tired.

"Nothing in the next few hours at least," Gruar replied. "The message will have to work its way back to someone who can press the right button, and then the alternative plans will have to get moving. It's really better that they try Channel Z : I'd rather catch them."

"Why is Channel Z so important?" Alasdair asked. "Is there a record of the Craggan conference being smuggled out?"

"I wonder. I think that's what we're meant to think. I first got on to Craggan and Wynrame because I was trying to trace the spy route to Dounreay. The conference was just a nuisance, as far as I was concerned. Then we found the dead man, and I began to wonder if I was wrong. Remember our tour of the lodge?"

"Yes," Alasdair said. "You picked up these pieces of wire."

"Right. I took care to see what I was meant to see. That business about the window cords was a bluff and I let Wynrame see that it was. But I also had a good look at the conference room. There were two microphones there—one in the blocked-off bookshelves, and one in the base of that armchair you so kindly moved for me. So I wondered rather more." He paused to stub out his cigarette. "We got rid of these microphones, naturally, and kept watching. They haven't been replaced, and we're pretty certain that the conference hasn't been tapped.

But why? One man is dead, but the other is still in the neighbourhood, and he certainly wasn't sent to do nothing. So I'm inclined to think that the bluff was a good deal more elaborate than first appeared, and that Dounreay is still the target. My guess is that Channel Z is an emergency trapdoor on the Dounreay route, and that something important has been happening at one end or other of that route. I'm working on that basis. We may have broken the first link, but there's a lot to do yet before we put the whole chain out of action."

He stretched out in an armchair and drank some more coffee. Alasdair shivered in reaction. Where did Ann fit in? Was she another link to be broken? Had she taken him for a British agent? And what would happen to her if Gruar worked his operation successfully? He got up and padded round the room in a cold sweat of apprehension and self-reproach. Either he had been taken for a ride, and he had been a fool not to see it, or something important was going to be destroyed.

Gruar looked at him as he circled the room.

"Look here, Alasdair," he said at last. "There are still one or two things to be worked out. Remember that someone killed the first agent, and we still don't know who did it. Cattanach means to get that cleared up. It's ludicrous in a way, worrying about the death of a spy, but I see why he's doing it. And that suits me. I'd like to know who did the killing, though I wouldn't guarantee to tell Cattanach if I did find out. But I think you'll be relieved when he finally gets there, as he probably will tomorrow."

"I'm making a fool of myself," was Alasdair's only comment.

"If you mean about the woman, then forget it. A lot of men do that, some of them more than once. I do it myself, and it doesn't hurt any the less each time. But, if you mean about the dead man, then you may be right. There's a clue somewhere, and nobody has spotted it yet. That's why I'm going to give Cattanach his head tomorrow. And if you stop to think, the last person to do it would be another Russian agent."

Gruar could have meant Erica Hakonson, but Alasdair didn't bother to ask. What Gruar had said didn't really help. If Ann was an agent, then he'd been fooled and he had a lot to forget. If she wasn't an agent, what was she doing with Hakonson? He knew, suddenly and decisively, that he had to find out everything about her. Just as Gruar, for his different reasons, must know, so he had to know. No burden of proof: only moral certainty, enough to let him put what had happened on Invermudale sands in its proper place. That much he had to have. He looked at Gruar with sudden affection; it was, he realised, the first time he had done so.

CHAPTER TEN

"OBSTRUCTING the police, assaulting Constable Thomson, discharging a firearm recklessly, dangerous driving," said Inspector Cattanach. "A reasonable score. It's been enough to get McGlashan talking."

The Inspector was pleased with himself. He filled his pipe with elaborate care, watching a bus-load of tourists spill out on to the road in front of Dalbreck Abbey. A pair of seagulls, less tolerant onlookers, flapped discontentedly away and circled round the beaten sandstone walls of the roofless tower. On the far side of the square an old man was wheeling a barrow full of cabbages towards the Schivas Arms. Alasdair, remembering some remarkable meals he had endured in that grandiose but cheerless hotel, felt comfortably detached. This was one hazard at least that he could avoid.

"And what has McGlashan said?" Gruar asked. The mid-afternoon sun was hot on the wooden bench outside the police office, and he was soaking it up, his eyes half-closed and his legs sprawled forwards. He looked detached, uninterested, a polite audience for Cattanach. Alasdair, hot in his tweeds, elbows on his knees, wasn't deceived. In a few hours Channel Z would be opening, and Gruar would have work to do.

"Quite a lot," said Cattanach. "We know how the poaching ring works. Thomson was in it, and Wynrame, and half a dozen men in Glasgow. Right now the Glasgow police are asking them some questions, and they'll be wanting the right answers. The men are employees of Mr. Winesack, but I suppose that it's too much to expect that we'll get a lead back to him."

Two very large women got out of the bus. Fascinated, Alasdair saw that they were wearing scarlet dunce's caps on

143

which were inscribed the words "Kiss Me Quick". Their faces as red as their headgear, the women stood looking around. A dozen paces away Queen Victoria, swathed in yellow paint by a well-meaning Town Council, and wearing her Imperial crown, stared at them from the canopy of an exuberant cast-iron fountain. Thomson's broken body, humped impersonally under a tarpaulin on a station platform, was a whole world away.

"Did you show McGlashan the photographs of the drowned man?" asked Cattanach.

"Yes."

"What did he say?"

"What you guessed. He and his gang brought the man up to Rhintraid on Thursday night and dumped him on Thomson. They swear that's the first and the last they ever saw of him. They also say that they brought up another man as well. It wasn't the first time they've done this sort of ferrying."

"The man at the stable, I presume," Gruar said.

"I expect so. At any rate, they were up tonight to collect a return party and take them to Glasgow. The party was to be three strong."

Alasdair heard Gruar draw in his breath sharply and nod in satisfaction.

"Who gave McGlashan his orders?" he asked.

The Inspector looked angry.

"Thomson. They had a standard plan ready, if there was ever any trouble. Thomson was to put on a false show of chasing them. And of course there was always the poaching as a cover to what was going on."

"So McGlashan knew that the poaching was only a blind."

"I couldn't say it was as simple as that, Mr. Gruar. McGlashan's a poacher all right, and a dirty one, but, unless I'm very much mistaken, he believes that these men he carried were part of the poaching organisation."

"Which means that at least one person at the Glasgow end is involved in the spy route," Gruar said, half to himself.

"There's just one thing about McGlashan that puzzles me,"

said Cattanach. "He's carrying a lot of money—a couple of hundred pounds—which he insists is his own and has nothing to do with the poaching. I can't make out why he should say that. We couldn't take the money from him even if we could prove that it was his poaching profits."

"Odd," Gruar said. Alasdair sat still. An idea was beginning to take form. He watched the bus passengers straggle up the path to the Abbey. Half of his mind objected to the vista of over-filled tartan slacks; the other half was groping after something important.

"McGlashan talked pretty readily," Gruar went on. "You don't think he knows more than he's admitted about the drowned man?"

Cattanach shook his head.

"I don't think so. There's been no public suggestion of murder yet. In any case, McGlashan is much more worried about Thomson."

"Does he know Thomson is dead?" There was a flicker of amusement in Gruar's quick sideways glance.

"Oh yes," said Cattanach blandly. "He knows that all right. What he doesn't know is just where and when it happened."

Gruar didn't push the point any further. The method, Alasdair reflected, had been effective. What he hadn't expected was that Cattanach should be so unorthodox. He felt a stab of uneasiness. The Inspector was more formidable than he had realised.

Cattanach's pipe had gone out. He relit it carefully, cupping his hands to shield the bowl from the non-existent wind. He sat looking for a moment at the spent match, then flicked it away with his forefinger. He looked dissatisfied.

"There's still that money to be accounted for," he said. A sudden burst of anger showed on his face. "Damn that ugly black devil with his scar. I'll find out yet what——"

The idea that had been lurking in the depths of Alasdair's mind rose cleanly to the surface.

"Can I have a look at McGlashan?" he asked cautiously, getting to his feet.

K

Cattanach was off-hand.

"If you want to, I suppose. But I don't see how that's going to help."

"Just curiosity," he mumbled, avoiding Gruar's eye.

"All right. Go into the front office and ask Sergeant Ross to let you look through the hatch. The gang are being charged at this very minute."

One look was enough. Two of the three men were the pair who had been involved in the scuffle in the strath. The third was the scar-faced man who had been drinking with Naverack at Invermudale on Sunday.

"Yes, that's Joe McGlashan," Sergeant Ross said in answer to Alasdair's question.

Alasdair went back out into the sunlight and stood looking down at Cattanach.

"McGlashan was at Invermudale on Sunday," he said. "I saw him receiving money from Professor Naverack in the bar there."

"Did anyone else see this," Cattanach asked. He was less excited than Alasdair had expected.

"Wattie Jardine was with me in the bar, but I think he was too far away to see the money. It changed hands pretty quickly."

"Just so. Just so." Cattanach was silent for a long time before going on. "You're telling me, are you, that Professor Naverack was involved in the poaching? Or do you think that he is a spy?"

Alasdair shrugged.

"I'm just telling you what I saw."

"Of course. A pity nobody else saw it. A pity too"— Cattanach looked straight at Alasdair—"that you have reasons of your own for disliking the Professor."

The implication was clear. Alasdair had a motive for framing Naverack, and Cattanach was showing that he knew it.

Gruar filled the edgy silence that followed.

"The money does exist, of course," he said in a neutral tone.

"What if it does?" Cattanach flashed back at him. "That's no proof that Macvartney's story is true."

The tourists were coming out of the Abbey, their thirst for culture replaced by a hunger for the shops of Dalbreck. Alasdair watched them go. Cattanach's altar had waited too long for an offering, and the Inspector wouldn't be sorry to see Alasdair Macvartney as the sacrifice. Spies were one thing; a man with grudges, a man who slept with someone else's wife and hinted at links between poachers and university professors, was something very different. Again Alasdair had the uneasy feeling that somewhere, sometime, he had had a clue, a vital clue, in his grasp, and had failed to recognise it. Now he had got to find it urgently.

Gruar got to his feet.

"So the Procurator-Fiscal is on your tail, is he?" he said to Cattanach.

The Inspector looked black for a moment, then laughed.

"Just that. Just the matter of a tidy-minded lawyer—and an Inspector of Police who doesn't like having dead bodies in his county. Don't forget that, either of you."

If Gruar was annoyed at being coupled with Alasdair, he gave no sign of it. Instead, he looked at his watch.

"Three o'clock," he said. "Time you were on your way to Craggan, Inspector. You never got your questions asked yesterday. By tonight things may be too busy up there."

Cattanach tapped out the dead ashes of his pipe.

"You're right," he said. "Craggan it had better be for both of us. If you can spare the time"—he looked mildly at Alasdair as he spoke—"I'd like you to come with us, Macvartney."

The implication was clear. Alasdair nodded, without speaking. Beyond Cattanach's shoulder he could see a girl with black hair standing beside the bus. She reminded him of Ann, and he felt unhappy.

*   *   *

"Still in session, Mr. Gruar," said the young man with the

toothbrush moustache. He looked at his watch. "This meeting is scheduled to finish by six o'clock, and I don't expect it's going to run much over. Seems that even scientists like to fish sometimes."

"Twenty minutes," Gruar said to Cattanach. "We'll go into the office and wait."

The last time Alasdair had been in Craggan it had been empty and dead. Now there was a continuous hum of noise as they stood outside the front door. A typewriter rattled, a telephone bell rang insistently, there was a clatter of dishes from the kitchen quarters. Alasdair glanced up at the library. The windows were tight shut. He hoped the American scientists inside could survive an afternoon without air-conditioning.

Gruar led the way into the house. A polite voice wanted to see their passes. Cattanach grunted and complied. Sergeant Ross, who had driven the police car from Dalbreck, followed suit. Alasdair, bringing up the rear, produced his letter. The polite voice was unimpressed, and Gruar had to make an entry in a pass-book before the party could move on. He was replacing his pen in his pocket when the door of the library opened, and the conference members began to come down the stairs. Gruar stood back against the wall to let them pass; Alasdair flattened himself beside him and watched the faces. Crossrig was there, talking hard, oblivious as ever to his surroundings. Behind him came Hakonson—a tired Hakonson, the strain more clearly written on his face than when Alasdair had seen him down by the river.

The group passed and Alasdair relaxed. Cattanach, cap in hand, was looking round with reluctant curiosity. Sergeant Ross was staring stolidly at the floor. Gruar gestured to them.

"This way," he said, and moved across the hall towards the green baize door leading to the kitchen quarters. The two policemen followed, Alasdair behind them. He was almost at the door when more footsteps sounded on the stairs. Automatically he looked up. It was Naverack.

Recognition was instant and mutual. For a moment the Professor registered a mixture of emotions—surprise, embarrassment, dislike, almost fear. Then Alasdair was through the baize door. Gruar, aware that something had happened, was looking back speculatively at him. Alasdair answered the unspoken question.

"Naverack. He recognised me."

Cattanach's shoulders hunched ominously. Gruar, though, was pleased.

"Well, we'll see if there's any reaction to that. You'll be seeing the Professor soon enough yourself, Inspector. He won't run away."

Cattanach made no reply.

They entered what had once been the housekeeper's sitting-room. Now it was a jumble of tables and folding chairs, large scale maps and black metal boxes. To one side stood three telephones; in another corner was a radio transmitter. A man sitting before the telephones looked up briefly as the party came in. Gruar paid no attention to him. He pushed three chairs forward for his companions, and signed to them to sit down.

"Wait five minutes," he said to Cattanach, "and I'll arrange for you to see these people in the dining-room, Inspector."

In the uneasy silence that followed Gruar's departure Alasdair looked curiously round the room. Sergeant Ross too was inspecting it. What he saw clearly scandalised him. The paraphernalia of security was in sharp contrast to a coloured view of Balmoral, in a frame of heliotrope papier-maché heather, and a photograph of a severe clerical gentleman carrying a top hat. The profane had displaced the sacred, and Ross was resenting it. Cattanach stared at the floor, his eyes sombre.

It was a long five minutes, but at last Gruar was back, grinning.

"I've just had a message that Professor Naverack believes that amongst the house staff there is a man who was recently discharged from the employment of the University of Perth; he wonders if anyone is aware of this, and whether the man ought to be investigated."

Alasdair laughed and shot a glance at Cattanach. The Inspector looked back at him, his face a careful blank.

"What are you going to ask these people, Inspector?" Gruar said quickly.

"I want to review what they told me about their movements on Friday night. The more they can tell me, the easier it will be to find out just who had the time and the opportunity to kill the man."

"So you're sure now that it was murder?"

"As sure as I can be without definite evidence. Russian agents don't drown themselves in rivers the size of the Blackwater. I suppose it's possible that the spies had a fight, or that the dead man was a traitor, but that looks too easy an explanation. So we can rule out Wynrame and the mysterious Igor. This is how I see it, Mr. Gruar. That man was left with Thomson on Thursday night. He must have been brought to Craggan later. The most obvious time for that is Friday evening, when Thomson drove up to Craggan, collecting Wynrame in Halmidary on the way. We can time that visit pretty accurately, for Thomson was seen in Halmidary at 8.40."

Gruar nodded.

"Our man at the station confirms that, I know."

"Very well. In that case," Cattanach continued, his face reddening with triumph as he got into his stride, "we have to work out various people's movements between 8.55, the earliest time Thomson's car could have reached Craggan, and, for safety, 11.30, half an hour before you found the body. I'm going to hammer away at that. Something may turn up, some discrepancy that will give us a lead."

"I'll give you a suggestion, Inspector," Gruar said slowly.

"Which is—?"

"I think you can cut down the time involved if you remember to ask each of them about the rifle in the gunroom. I suggest you take it with you to the interviews and find out whether anyone saw it on Friday evening."

"I don't see how that's going to help me," Cattanach objected. "The man wasn't shot."

Gruar's explosion of temper was completely unexpected.

"Damn you, do as I say. If you find that out quickly, we'll

be ready for Channel Z when it starts moving. The rifle is significant. Do what I say, and I'll be able to tell you who could have murdered the man. But hurry up."

For a moment Cattanach was ready to resist. Then, with an effort, he held himself back.

"Just as you say." He got to his feet. "I'll hold you to that. Come on, Sergeant."

The policemen were at the door when Gruar spoke again.

"If you want to get Naverack straight," he said, "you could try to find out if he was being blackmailed by McGlashan."

The door closed. Gruar took a packet of cigarettes from his pocket. He threw one to Alasdair, lit another himself, and began to laugh softly.

"Time I stopped that sort of performance," he said. "It's not Cattanach's fault. I lose my temper once in every case, and this time he got it. He'd have been furious if the Procurator-Fiscal hadn't encouraged him to get a move on, for he's determined to find a murderer."

"He's pretty determined to find that I'm a murderer," Alasdair said grimly.

Gruar grinned.

"That's not entirely fair. At least, it won't be by the time he's listened to Naverack. Let's hear what's happening."

He reached up and switched on a small loudspeaker that hung from the wall. Through the crackling and hissing came Cattanach's voice, at once coarsened and sharpened by the machine.

"Come in, please, President. I'm sorry to disturb your afternoon."

Crossrig's public voice next, careful and deliberate, the voice of a man accustomed to talking to people of lesser intelligence.

"Not at all, Inspector. What can I do to help you?"

"Well, sir, we're reviewing the business of that man who was found drowned."

"Have you found out who the poor fellow was?" As he would speak of a student who had gone to the bad, thought Alasdair.

"Not yet, sir, but we have got a line to follow up. What we want to do now is to check some times. There are signs that someone suspicious was moving about the grounds that night, and it would help us if we could fix more closely the movements of the people who were staying in the lodge. Can you answer me a few questions on that? It would help me to put in a tidy report."

"Of course." Clever of Cattanach to appeal to the great man in this way; aid for underdeveloped brains—a line sure to catch Crossrig.

"Thank you. Now, sir, we already know that you went down to Halmidary with Professor and Mrs. Hakonson and Professor Naverack at 7.20. You left the Halmidary hotel around 8.35 and drove back here. And after that?"

"I'm quite clear on what I did. In my position I have to keep to a rigid timetable, as you will understand, Inspector, so I tend always to watch the time. Let me see. Yes. We were back in the house by 8.50. I went to my room and wrote up some notes for the conference. When I had finished I went downstairs. It was almost dark by then. I remember that, for I looked at my watch and realised that I had been writing for nearly two hours."

"What time was that, President?"

"10.45."

"And then?"

"I felt that I wanted some fresh air before going to bed, so I went into the cloakroom to collect my scarf, which I had left there. Then I went out on to the lawn. After about five minutes Professor Hakonson joined me."

"Did you see where he came from?"

"No. But he said he had heard me going out, and suggested we might go for a short walk. So we went down to the river and along to the wire bridge."

"Just so. I'm told you met Mr. Gruar, Wynrame the keeper, and Macvartney the watcher there sometime between 11.20 and 11.30."

"Correct, Inspector. We took a few minutes crossing the

bridge, for I recall wondering if I would fall off. I don't indulge in that sort of exercise normally, you see."

"But you didn't fall off, sir?"

"Oh no, neither of us did. I was quite relieved."

"And after that?"

"We walked to the farm, and home up the road. I was in my bedroom just before midnight."

"I see. That's very clear, sir. Thank you. Now, you saw nothing odd—no stranger, for instance—all evening?"

"Only the river watcher who met us at the bridge. I've forgotten his name."

"Thank you, President. One last point. Did you notice anything unusual in the hall as you went out? I'm just wondering if the dead man might have been hanging around in the hope of stealing something."

"No. I don't think so."

"There wasn't a weapon of any kind there—something like this rifle, for example?"

"A gun? Wait—yes, there was. That gun you're holding was on the hall table when we came back from Halmidary."

"And was it there when you came downstairs to go for your walk?"

A pause.

"No. It wasn't. I expect somebody put it back in the gun-room. Professor Naverack has been using it quite often. You could ask him."

"Quite so, quite so. Well, I'll not keep you any longer, sir. And perhaps you'll consider this interview confidential. I'll have to give the Fiscal a report, you see."

"Certainly, Inspector. Good-bye."

"Good-bye, sir. And thank you."

A door opened, then closed again, its sound magnified by the loudspeaker.

"Right, Sergeant." It was Cattanach's voice. "We've got all that straight. Go and get either Professor Hakonson or his wife. We'll leave Naverack to the last."

Alasdair got up from his chair and prowled round the room.

The silent man at the telephones glanced curiously at him, then began to adjust a squat black box on the table. He pulled on a pair of headphones and listened. After a few seconds he called softly to Gruar.

"Transatlantic call, sir—outwards. Shall I record it?"

Gruar nodded.

"I can guess who that is," he said, half to himself.

The loudspeaker crackled again.

"Professor Hakonson, sir," came Sergeant Ross's voice. "Mrs. Hakonson is making a telephone call."

Alasdair saw the satisfaction in Gruar's face. Then the loudspeaker took his attention again.

"You want to see me, Inspector?" It was Hakonson, brash, assured, transatlantic.

"If you can spare me a few minutes, sir." Cattanach was polite.

"Carry on. But make it short. I've a date right now—with a fishing rod."

"Of course, sir. You won't catch much tonight, I'm afraid. There isn't enough water in the river."

"Enough for what I want." The confidence in Hakonson's voice was very apparent. "So get on with it."

"Surely. I just want to review your movements last Friday night, sir. We're trying to pin down this man who was drowned. He may have been trying to break into the lodge, so the more evidence we have about times the better. Now, you went to Halmidary with the rest of the guests here?"

"Correct, Inspector." Hakonson was quieter now.

"When did you get back?"

"Just before nine o'clock, I reckon. We left the hotel about 8.30."

"And then?"

"Let's get this straight. I took the car round to the garage, came back into the house, and read a book in the library. Round about a quarter off eleven I heard President Crossrig go downstairs and out the front door. I reckoned some fresh air was a sound idea, so I went after him. We walked through the woods to that goddam wire bridge, met the game warden and two others there, then came home."

"Can you fix any times?"

"No. Not until we got back. The clock in the hall said 11.50 when we came in."

"Did you see anything or anyone strange when you were outside?"

"Only these men at the bridge. I'd never seen them before, but the game warden told us their names."

"Did you see this rifle anywhere that evening?"

Scraping of metal on wood.

"Say, that's a wicked piece of hardware, Inspector. I think the warden takes one like it when he's out on his patrols. I've seen Naverack practising with one too. Now that you ask, it was on the table in the hall on Friday night. I saw it there when I went out after the President. It wasn't there when I got back, though."

"Are you sure of that, Professor?"

"One hundred per cent. Why?"

"We've got a report that one like it was stolen not so very far away. The dead man may have been involved."

"He sure had a good taste in guns, if he did. Anything else you want to ask?"

"No, sir. That's all. Thank you very much. And good fishing."

"Thanks, Inspector. Good-bye."

Again the sound of the door. A match scratched.

"Sir?" It was Sergeant Ross's voice.

"Yes?"

"Something wrong about that rifle. These stories don't fit."

"Damn it, of course I've noticed that, man. But tell me what it means, if you can."

Gruar chuckled.

"That's got him thinking at last," he said.

Alasdair was thinking too, but not about the rifle. There was another discrepancy somewhere. Something had happened on Friday night, something that nobody else had spotted.

He opened his mouth to speak, but Gruar waved him to silence.

"Here's the prize exhibit," he said. "Let's hear how Cattanach takes him."

The loudspeaker came alive again.

"Good afternoon, Inspector. How can I help you today?" It was Naverack at his most genial, spreading sweetness and light; but too effusive, too anxious to please, too uneasy underneath it all.

Cattanach's attack was direct.

"Professor Naverack, have you ever met a man called Joseph McGlashan?"

A hiss of breath being drawn sharply in. A pause.

"No, Inspector, not that I know of. Who is he?"

"He is the leader of a gang of deer poachers from Perth. You were seen meeting him in the hotel at Invermudale on Sunday afternoon, when you handed him a considerable sum of money."

"You're mistaken, Inspector."

"Are you sure, Professor?" Cattanach's voice was beginning to rise. "There's a witness—the man you were complaining about half an hour ago."

"It would be him. Lies, lies, the whole story. Can't you see, Inspector, that that man has a grudge against me? I helped to get him sacked from the University. He spent his time seducing other men's wives. He——"

"Just one wife, according to our reports," Cattanach said dryly. "Was McGlashan blackmailing you?"

"I don't know what you mean, Inspector."

"Then I'll tell you. Joseph McGlashan and two others were arrested at Dalbreck last night. They have been charged with shooting at a policeman, illegal possession of firearms, and various other things. McGlashan has made a statement, admitting that he has been responsible for a number of poaching raids in this county. He has named various people who were also involved. Some of these are employed by Mr. Winesack, who is, I believe, a friend of yours. In addition, McGlashan had two hundred pounds in his pockets when we arrested him. So you'd be as well to tell us anything you know, Professor."

This time the silence was a long one. When Naverack finally spoke it was the voice of a different man.

"I've nothing to tell you, Inspector."

"Yes, you have." Cattanach was shouting now, pushing home his attack. The loudspeaker rattled at the violence in his voice. "You'd better realise that there may be more than poaching involved. There's a dead man still to be identified, and now Constable Thomson from Rhintraid has been killed. You're walking on dangerous ground, Professor Naverack, and it'll take more than President Crossrig to get you away from it unless you answer my questions. Was McGlashan blackmailing you?"

It worked. Naverack, Alasdair realised, had always been a shell, a man who found it easiest to do what others asked him. Now he was paying the price. The words began to pour out.

"Yes, he was. But it was nothing to do with killing anybody, I swear, Inspector. I never saw the drowned man in my life. And I never had anything to do with any poaching."

"How did McGlashan come to know you?"

"Because I once passed on some money to him. I didn't know what it was for, but my friend Winesack asked me to do it. And I couldn't refuse him, could I? After all, he's a very dear friend, and he pays for my salary at Perth. I haven't done anything illegal. I've just handed over some money for a friend."

Gruar screwed up his face as the words tumbled out of the loudspeaker.

"Why was McGlashan blackmailing you? Why didn't you come to the police about him?"

"It had nothing to do with Winesack or the poaching, I promise you. It was just something—private."

"I can guess." The contempt in Cattanach's voice was blatant now. "Well, I won't chase that any further now. I've got more important things to think about. I want you to answer some questions about Friday night—and this time you'd better tell the truth straight off."

"All right." The relief in Naverack's tone was very obvious. A lot of young men at the University of Perth are going to be spared something from now on, Alasdair thought. He found himself half-sympathising with Naverack; being suspected by Cattanach wasn't amusing.

"Your movements on Friday night, from the time you left the Halmidary hotel—as precisely as you are able, with as many times as you can remember," Cattanach was saying.

"Yes. I drove back from Halmidary to Craggan." Naverack's voice was flat, mechanical. "It was 8.50 when we got here. Professor Hakonson said he would put the car away in the garage, so I went into the house. I went up to my room and wrote some business letters—to my bank manager, to my insurance agent, to——"

"All right. That's not important. Did you leave your room again?"

"Yes. I remembered that just before we went to Halmidary I had taken out the stalking rifle from the gun-room, so I went downstairs to put it away."

"Is this the rifle?"

"Yes. I've been amusing myself target shooting with it, and I had been intending to take it out again that evening. Then we decided to go to Halmidary, so I left it lying on the hall-table. I saw it there when we came back."

"When did you recall that it was still there?"

"Just before 9.45. I know that, because I looked at my watch and thought about going to bed. It was then that I remembered the rifle."

"And did you put it back in the gun-room?"

"No. It wasn't on the table any more."

"Did you look in the gun-room?"

"Yes. It wasn't there either."

"And then?"

"I thought that someone else had taken it out—Wynrame perhaps. Next morning I had another look in the gun-room, and found that it had been returned. I never gave it another thought after that."

"I see. Was there anyone else about when you came down-stairs?"

"Only Mrs. Hakonson. She was just going out for a stroll. She asked me to go with her, but I was tired and I wanted to go to bed. I don't like women."

Gruar grimaced at the words, then grinned at Alasdair.

"After that?" said Cattanach.

"I went to bed."

"And nobody saw you until Saturday morning at break-fast?"

"That's right." Naverack's voice was unhappy.

"Just so. Not very helpful for us—or for you, Professor Naverack," Cattanach said. "You'd better go now. I'll maybe want to ask you some more questions later."

"What do you mean—not very helpful to me?" The panic was very evident now.

"Just that. You've been keeping odd company, Professor, so you mustn't be surprised if you attract a bit of attention."

"What are you going to do about McGlashan blackmailing me?"

"Something. Or just possibly nothing. Now go, please."

Gruar reached up and switched off the loudspeaker. The silent man at the telephone detached a sheet of paper from the side of the black box and handed it to Gruar. Gruar read it slowly, then reached for a telephone.

"Inspector? I suggest you postpone seeing Mrs. Hakonson for the moment and come back here. I've something to show you. Right? Yes, I'll explain about the rifle now."

Cattanach came through the door at speed, Sergeant Ross trailing after him, a bundle of closely-written sheets in his hands.

"All right," Gruar said. "Don't bother to tell us. We were listening in."

Cattanach's face reddened. He glared at Gruar for a second, then bellowed with laughter. Alasdair felt the tension dissolving away. Whatever Cattanach had felt about him, whatever he still suspected, things were going to be easier now.

"Too much science here for me," the Inspector said. "Well, what's this you want to show me?"

Gruar waved the sheet of paper in front of him.

"To save time, I'll cut it short. Mrs. Hakonson has just been on the telephone to a firm of lawyers in Baltimore, U.S.A. She has instructed them to start divorce proceedings against her husband, and she is flying back to America from Prestwick on Thursday—alone."

Cattanach rubbed his moustache.

"Do you tell me that? I'd better talk to her as soon as I can."

"I don't think it's necessary. You've found out enough to go on already, haven't you?"

"You mean about the rifle?"

"Precisely."

"I don't see what you're getting at. The stories about it don't tally, but I don't know where that gets us."

"Listen, then." Gruar lit a cigarette, and leaned back in his chair. "That rifle was left lying in the hall here. It was still there at 8.50, when the party came back from Halmidary. The next time it was seen for certain was at 11.30, when Alasdair and I saw Wynrame carrying it at the wire bridge."

"Steady. Are you sure that was the same rifle?"

"Wynrame told me on Saturday that he didn't have a rifle, but took the lodge one when he needed it. He didn't say that he had it on Friday night, but I saw him with it. That was the first thing that worried me. He must have had a reason for carrying it. It wasn't to shoot vermin, for if he wanted to do that he would have used his own shotgun. He took the rifle, either because the dead man had gone missing, or because he had found the body and realised that it was a matter of murder."

"But why risk being seen at the lodge? Wouldn't he have a revolver of his own?" Cattanach objected.

"Maybe. Russian agents aren't encouraged to wander around with revolvers when it isn't strictly necessary. Thomson was pretty desperate when he used his last night. But Wynrame could carry a gun openly—as long as it was the sort of gun a keeper would use. It was just unfortunate for him that we spotted that it was a stalking-rifle."

Cattanach's face lit up suddenly. Watching him, Alasdair was reminded of the large men in kilts he had seen at the Dalbreck Highland Games. Big men, red-faced and sweating, straining at the fifty-six-pound weight, then all at once jerking it up, so that it flew easily and cleanly over a bar higher than their own heads. Cattanach was seeing it all fall into place.

"Which means that we can cut down the critical time quite a lot," he burst out. "Whatever happened to the dead man happened before 9.45, when Naverack found that the rifle was missing. Mrs. Hakonson may be able to give us a check there, but I think Naverack was too scared to tell lies. Now, does that rule anyone out——"

He stopped suddenly and looked at Alasdair.

"It rules you out, Macvartney. You were in Halmidary village at 8.40, you were seen at the station at 9.25. You don't have wings, do you?"

Cattanach spoke gruffly, avoiding Alasdair's eyes. Alasdair was content to leave it at that. He wasn't looking for apologies. That wasn't the way of the strath. But he knew that, once convinced, Cattanach would never misjudge him again. In an oblique, unacknowledged way, this was the first step towards acceptance. He could never be quite an outsider in the strath again. And that made it harder still to think about Ann.

"Go on, Inspector," Gruar said, glancing at his watch. "You can get a little further still."

"Yes, I can." Cattanach's voice was hard now. "The gun was gone when Crossrig went out at 10.45. Both he and Naverack agree that it had gone. But Hakonson said that he saw it in the hall, though he went out after Crossrig did. In other words, he was lying—he must have gone out before the gun was taken, before 9.45, if we believe Naverack, before the man died. Which means——"

The words died away. The room had become very quiet. Cattanach looked at the floor. At last he raised his head and stared at Gruar.

L

"Proof? Motive? There's not enough to go on in this. I can't risk getting my feet wet over this case——"

Alasdair interrupted him. The missing piece was sliding into place.

"Wet feet. That's what I couldn't remember. Will wet feet do for evidence, Inspector?"

"What do you mean?"

"Just this. When I met Crossrig, Hakonson and Wynrame at the wire bridge, Hakonson's feet were wet—in fact, he was soaking up to the knees. I suppose that I imagined that he had slipped off the wire, if I thought about it at all. But Crossrig was quite definite just now that they both got across without accident; and they both said that they simply walked down from the lodge to the bridge. Yet Hakonson's trousers were soaked while Crossrig's were dry. If you want a discrepancy, Inspector, there's one for you."

"Which means," Gruar cut in, "that Hakonson was out of the lodge at a time when he claimed to be in the library."

"It's not evidence, not evidence to convict a man, Mr. Gruar," Cattanach said slowly. "And where am I going to get the evidence?"

"You can search this house," said Gruar. "Look at it like this. By ten o'clock on Friday night there was a lot happening out in the woods. Macvartney and Mrs. Wynrame saw someone on the move down near the bridge. I was up having a look at the lodge myself, and I had to go to ground twice. Then there was that stone in the road that ditched Mrs. Jardine's car. My guess is that Wynrame put it there to give himself warning of any vehicle turning up. It all adds up. Wynrame and his friend Igor were thoroughly alarmed and on the hunt for something. We know that the dead man was one of their crew. The only person who has told us a provable lie about his movements is Hakonson. If you think the man was murdered, then you'd better get hold of Hakonson."

"And the motive? I'm not having anyone killed in this county, even if he is a Russian spy, and the murderer getting away with it. Show me a motive, and I'll get after Hakonson."

Gruar looked at the man beside the telephones.

"Any word of the Oslo courier?" he asked.

"The plane landed at Wick at five o'clock. He should be here any minute now."

Alasdair stiffened. Another strand was beginning to fall into place. Before he could speak a telephone rang. The silent man picked it up and listened, then turned to Gruar.

"The courier has just checked in at the outer guard-point," he said.

"Good." Gruar looked less pleased than he sounded. Alasdair caught a quick flicker of his eyes. "I hope I can give you some sort of motive now."

The courier was a small, harassed man with a large brief case. He handed it to Gruar, laid a receipt form in front of him, then went out without speaking.

"That job would drive me crazy," Gruar said, breaking open the heavy seals on the case. He reached inside it, pulled out an envelope, and slit it open. The contents fell on to the table. Gruar picked up a typewritten sheet of paper and studied it. Alasdair could see three photographs lying face downwards on the table. Behind him he could hear Cattanach's heavy breathing as the Inspector craned forward.

"This is it," Gruar said at last. "A Norwegian Intelligence report. Leif Hakonson emigrated in 1945 under American Government auspices—we know that already. What we didn't know was that he had previously had a quarrel with his elder brother Eric, also a scientist. The quarrel is believed to have been over Eric's Scottish-born wife, who left her husband and went to America with Leif. Norwegian Intelligence lost contact with Eric four months later, when he left his university post. He hasn't been spotted since officially, but there was a report two years ago from the Norwegian consul at Jakarta that someone very like him had turned up in a Russian scientific mission there."

"It wasn't the present Mrs. Hakonson who went to America, I presume," said Cattanach.

"No. That all-American blonde is Leif Hakonson's third wife," replied Gruar.

He let his hand rest on the photographs. He was, Alasdair sensed, reluctant to display them.

"What are these?" Cattanach said impatiently.

Gruar turned one over and took his hand away.

"Leif Hakonson in 1944," he said. "Quite recognisable."

He laid the other photographs beside the first.

"And his brother Eric."

Alasdair knocked his chair back as he stumbled to his feet. There was something very close to compassion in Gruar's eyes as he watched him.

One photograph was of the drowned man, stripped of twenty years of ageing and conflict. The identification was inescapable. But it was something else that brought Alasdair to his feet. Ann Wynrame's face, younger but unmistakable, was staring up at him from the third photograph. He hardly heard Gruar's words.

"Eric Hakonson had a daughter. She was nine when her father disappeared, and she hasn't been seen since."

CHAPTER ELEVEN

"THE motive will do," Cattanach said quietly. "Good old-fashioned stuff, even if it seems to have worked in reverse. I want another talk with Hakonson. Sex—a very good motive. The revenger comes back after fifteen years—very good indeed. But he doesn't get his revenge; he gets killed instead—very dramatic. Yes, I'm going to see Hakonson again. Come on, Sergeant."

"He's on the river, isn't he?" said Gruar.

"At the Devil's Pool, I expect," Cattanach replied from the doorway. "I'll try down there first."

He paused, and turned abruptly. Sergeant Ross, hurrying behind, skidded to a halt, boots grinding on the linoleum-covered floor. He pulled at the peak of his cap and looked reproachfully at his superior.

"There's Mrs. Wynrame to think of," Cattanach began, then stopped as he saw Alasdair's face.

"Why?" Gruar said.

Cattanach opened his mouth to speak, then closed it again.

"Perhaps you're right," he said at last. "Hakonson's the man I'm after. What about his room? Can you have it searched for me?"

"Yes," said Gruar. He turned to the man at the table. "Alan, arrange for that, will you?"

Alan nodded, and picked up a telephone. Cattanach hesitated, then went out, Sergeant Ross trailing at his heels.

Gruar lit a cigarette and pushed the packet across the table. Alasdair let it lie. He picked up the three photographs and shuffled them from hand to hand.

"You knew there was a connection between Mrs. Wynrame and Hakonson, didn't you?" Gruar asked.

165

"Why do you think that?" Alasdair said.

"I saw you looking at that postcard in Hakonson's room on Saturday. I imagine that you saw the picture of the same valley in Wynrame's house. I did, when I paid a private visit on my own account on Sunday."

Alasdair tossed the photographs on to the table.

"All right. So I guessed it. What then?"

Gruar tapped the ash from his cigarette.

"Then, my guess is that you drew the wrong conclusions. Probably Mrs. Hakonson helped you to draw them."

"What conclusions would you have drawn?" Alasdair felt himself becoming angry.

"The ones that I did draw. Like you, I was sure the place was somewhere in Europe, not across the Atlantic. So I put some questions to Oslo. The results are on the table."

Alasdair turned away and walked to the window. Cattanach and Ross were trudging across the lawn towards the river. He pressed his fingers hard against the window-frame, feeling the bleached wood split under his nails.

"This is the story," Gruar said, after a pause. "Hakonson's brother came back as a Russian agent. The plan probably was for him to listen in to the conference, then get out again with McGlashan. That's why I was pleased when McGlashan said that he was to collect three passengers. Two from Craggan—Igor and Hakonson's brother—and therefore only one from Dounreay. So it all made sense. Eric Hakonson came back to do a job of work. He was lucky, he was going to see his daughter too. Probably they hadn't met for several years. It was a bit of a risk, though I've known the Russians take as big ones before. But instead he met his brother, by what must have been a complete accident, and got himself killed. So the plan to listen in to the conference had to be abandoned. Wynrame was clever there. He let us see enough to keep our eyes on this place, and so divert some of our attention from Dounreay. However, it didn't work out quite neatly enough. Last night we blocked the escape line. Igor is still here, and anyone involved at Dounreay is lying very low."

"And now?" Alasdair's anger was turning into curiosity.

"Now Channel Z is scheduled to open. Everybody is getting out—Wynrame, Igor, someone from Dounreay probably, and" —he hesitated—"Mrs Wynrame too."

"Does she know who killed her father?" Alasdair asked.

Gruar shrugged.

"She probably does," Alasdair went on, answering his own question. "I told her about Hakonson's trousers being wet."

Gruar stubbed out his cigarette and got to his feet.

"She's an agent too. You realise that?"

Alasdair swung round sharply, his anger flaring up again.

"Of course I realise it, damn you."

"But that isn't why you've been ready to help us, is it?" Gruar persisted.

"No, it isn't." Alasdair rode down hard on his resentment. "I'm helping you because I don't like Wynrame. I'm helping you because it gives me a chance to feel superior, gives me a chance to score over people like Cattanach. I'm helping you because——"

"Go on," Gruar said.

"Because I want that woman out of here. I told you as much in Inverness. I wasn't sure then. I'm sure now. I don't enjoy being made love to just because it suits an espionage time-table. And this is as far as I'm going. Get on with it yourself."

He turned back to the window and stared out at the blood-red decadence of the fuchsias. He was suddenly very tired and uninterested in the whole affair.

"I can tell you a little more before you go," Gruar said, in a business-like voice. "This is what is going to happen tonight. I've taken most of my men away from the lodge itself, apart from one who is tailing Wynrame. Now we're watching all the outlet points—the railway, the roads above and below Halmidary, the Cornessie path. There are also troops and police ready in an outer ring. Sometime in the next five hours or so Wynrame is going to make a break. We'll let him get started, let him pick up the rest of his party—and then we'll clean up."

"You're certain that Dounreay is involved?" Alasdair said.

It wasn't important and he wasn't interested, but he asked the question all the same.

"What's the alternative? Unless we're all fools, they haven't got anything out of this conference here. And don't forget that McGlashan was to collect three people."

"What about Hakonson?"

"Leave him to the police. I don't imagine Cattanach will find enough evidence to stick, but he can get on with the job. There's nothing in Hakonson's room to help. I know that, for we've been through his luggage ourselves already. No, Hakonson will get a fright, and that's about all. He'll have to pick up a new woman when he gets back to the States, but I shouldn't imagine he'll find another blonde very hard to come by."

"You don't think he's in any danger here?"

Gruar didn't answer at once.

"He might be. It doesn't do to rule out the personal factor. Mrs. Wynrame has enough reason to hate him, and she's certainly been keeping some sort of watch on him. But that could just be to make sure that he doesn't say anything about the dead man. I presume they banked on him being too scared to go to the police, and it looks as if they were right. Leave Hakonson to Cattanach. By tomorrow the spies will be in the net, or fifty miles out to sea. There are three Russian freighters just outside territorial waters off the North coast this evening."

Alasdair walked to the door. He was at the end of the line. Already Ann Wynrame was out of his life. Hakonson was going, Crossrig and Naverack were going, soon Gruar would go. Then there would be only the salmon left—the salmon and the ivory tower at Corrachan. It was time he went back there.

A telephone rang twice. Alan picked it up, listened, scribbled on a pad in front of him, and pushed the message across to Gruar. Gruar read the note, crumpled the paper up, and tossed it across the room.

"Here we go," he said to Alasdair. "Wynrame has slipped his tail somewhere between the kennels and the river."

He pulled open a drawer and took out a squat black automatic pistol and a box of ammunition. Alasdair watched him.

Under his apathy a small searing pain struck and struck again. There was going to be shooting, people were going to be hurt, Ann was going to be hurt. He stamped on the pain, buried it oceans deep.

Gruar was studying a map on the wall.

"Do you want to come with me?" he said over his shoulder.

"No," Alasdair replied. "I'm going home to Corrachan."

"Good idea. This is professionals' work now." Gruar's attention was clearly elsewhere. He was writing fast, passing notes to Alan, who was playing a complex solo on the three telephones. Alasdair pulled the door open. He had one foot in the passage outside when a thought came to him, and he shut the door again.

"Are you watching Corrachan?" he asked.

Gruar shook his head.

"No. It's a dead end, except for hill paths, and we've put men at all the exits from these. If Wynrame breaks clean away tonight, then I suppose the army can get blisters tomorrow by combing the hills, but that's not much of an idea. We collect tonight, or we don't collect at all. You'll find two guards at the stone bridge just before the hill up at Corrachan, but that's all."

"I'll tell you one last thing, then," Alasdair said. "I meant to tell you yesterday, but too much was happening. Someone has cached two fuel drums underwater at the top end of Loch Skiag."

Gruar stopped writing and turned round.

"Are you sure?"

"I broke an oar on one of them yesterday morning. Does it mean anything to you?"

"It could do—a launch, no, a plane or a helicopter, yes. And there are three Russian ships less than thirty miles away. Things happen to you, don't they, Alasdair?"

Gruar got to his feet and wandered round the room, whistling a pipe tune under his breath.

"We're watching these ships already, of course," he went on. "There's an Air Force patrol on the job right now. We'll call them up and pass this news on. Their orders are to let anything that comes from the ships fly inland, then to get it down over the sea, as near to the coast as possible, on the return journey."

"Will they shoot?" Alasdair asked.

"If need be. This isn't a time for asking too many questions."

The pain seared again. Something must have showed in his face, for Gruar strode across the room and took him by the shoulders.

"Time to go back to Corrachan, Alasdair," he said. "If you're still worrying about the woman, forget it—forget it for good this time. She went down to the farm for eggs and milk an hour ago. Mrs. Jardine tells us that she didn't stay more than ten minutes. Since then she hasn't been seen. I'm not going to kick you in the teeth, but forget her. You've been caught up in something big and nasty, and you're lucky to get out of it clean. One of my own men is dead already. Forget her. You don't really want to, but you haven't any choice. We'll go out on the river on Friday, when it's all over, and I'll tell you then what happened. But now get back to Corrachan and keep your head down."

He opened the door, pushed Alasdair out, and slammed it shut again.

*   *   *

It was almost eight o'clock. The sun was low in the sky. Down in the south-west a shoal of clouds was sprawling upwards like dark blue jellyfish. There was thunder in the air, heavy and ominous.

Alasdair walked down the hill towards the farm. He was out of the game. Cattanach was pursuing Hakonson up and down the river bank, Gruar was weaving his complicated magic in the lodge, and somewhere in the shimmering woods Ann Wynrame was on her way to Moscow. But he was out of the game.

In the farmhouse kitchen Mrs. Jardine was baking at the

range, and Wattie was cleaning a pair of boots. The kettle was steaming, and a collie was sleeping in front of the fire.

"Come away in, Alasdair," Mrs. Jardine said. "It's long enough since we saw you. Sit down and I'll make the tea. You'll be hungry?"

Alasdair nodded, and sprawled into a chair, letting tiredness sweep over him. It was good to be away from Gruar, good to be back among people who accepted him. There wasn't much else that was good in life, but this would do to be going on with. It was better than thinking of Ann, better than remembering the sound of the waves and her hair against the hot golden sand. If only he could creep inside the narrow shell of the strath, if only he could stop being a stranger in the one place he wanted to stay in. It would be easier once Ann had gone—or was dead among the conger eels and the sea-wrack out beyond Invermudale Bay.

When the tea came he found that he wasn't hungry. He sat looking at the fire. The collie, sensing his stare, whined uneasily and crept under the table.

"You're worried, Alasdair," said Mrs. Jardine gently, "and I'm thinking I know why. It's Ann Wynrame, isn't it?"

"It was, I suppose," Alasdair replied, "but that's past now. I'll not be seeing her again."

"A pity that. She's a nice lassie, though I'll not say as much for her husband. You're maybe sensible to take it that way, though."

Wattie cleared his throat. His wife glared at him, but he waved her silent.

"It's not my business, Alasdair. The wife aye tells me that if I'm a man among sheep I'm still a sheep among men. But I've never rightly known if we Scots are being sensible when we do what the kirk tells us, or whether we're not just being scared. I hope you're not being scared."

It was the look in the farmer's eyes that startled Alasdair. First MacAra, now Wattie: first the rake, now the respectable man. It was incitement, it was incurable sentimentality—or what was it? Suddenly he knew something, knew it with

absolute certainty. He wanted Ann, and he had been helping
to have her caught as a spy. What Gruar had said to him wasn't
false. It was only irrelevant.

And now it was too late. Or was it? There was one thing he
could still do. He could go to Corrachan, then row up to the
head of the loch. If he was right, and Gruar was wrong, that
was where the escape was going to happen. Perhaps he could
still be in time.

He stood up.

"Wattie, can I borrow the truck, please, to take the cow up
to Corrachan? It's about time I went back there."

Wattie looked him full in the face. What he saw seemed to
satisfy him, for he nodded agreement.

"Right you are, Alasdair. I'll fetch the beast for you."

*   *   *

A mile beyond the lodge, the guards at the stone bridge were
being relieved. Alasdair waited until the Landrover had passed
him on its way back to Craggan, then drove the truck up to the
end of the bridge. The cow was stamping uneasily behind him,
sensing the thunder coming and not liking it; the sooner he
had her back in her own byre at Corrachan the better. Across
the bridge the road ran transversely up a long open hill-face,
high above the river. Viewed from the bottom, it made sense
of Gruar's confidence. A skilled stalker might be able to work
his way across that face without being seen by a watcher at the
bridge, but Alasdair doubted it; a party of any size could never
hope to escape notice.

One of the new pair of guards examined his pass, folded
it, and handed it back. Alasdair was on the point of slipping
the truck into gear when the second guard called to him.

"That man's hooked a fish, hasn't he?"

Alasdair switched off and climbed out. He walked to the
parapet of the bridge and looked over. Two hundred yards
downstream the Blackwater tumbled down a rocky ledge into
a wide, swirling pool. The far bank was a sheer, unclimbable

slab of grey rock, along whose foot the current swept fast and deep. On the near bank heather and bracken ran waist-high down to a long gravel shoal.

A man was standing on the gravel. Alasdair had seen him before. It was Hakonson—Hakonson with a rod in his hands and a fish on the end of his line. Inspector Cattanach hadn't caught the American. Instead, Hakonson was catching a salmon —on a falling river, with an absurdly light rod, and with obviously very little idea of what to do about it.

Alasdair grinned. Behind him the cow grunted in complaint. Cattanach would be lucky if he found Hakonson before the rain came. Nobody who knew anything of the river would ever have thought of fishing that particular pool in its present condition. The picture of an irate Cattanach cutting his way through the evening midges, with Sergeant Ross suffering at his heels, pleased him. He turned back to the truck, still grinning.

"Why not go down and help him?" said one of Gruar's men. "He looks as if he could do with it."

Alasdair considered for a moment. He had no real wish to see any more of Hakonson. The man was almost certainly a murderer, and the police wanted to talk to him. On the other hand, he was fishing badly. Alasdair winced as the salmon broke surface in a long plunging jump; the way Hakonson handled his rod, it was a miracle that the line hadn't snapped. Nobody could be allowed to fish as badly as that, even someone he had once cuckolded. He had to get to Corrachan before the rain, but this would take ten minutes, no more.

"Right. I'll go and grass the fish for him," he said, and swung his feet over the parapet.

Hakonson looked up with relief as Alasdair slithered through the bracken.

"Glad to see you," he said. "What the heck do I do now? This isn't like hunting a swordfish from a swivel-seat."

Alasdair eyed the light cane trout rod, no more than nine foot long. The strain was telling on it.

"Give him some line when he tries to run," he said. "If you

hold on to the reel like that something will go. And get the point higher. Put pressure on the butt and you'll tire him out."

The fish was in a hurry. Thrice in quick succession he swung downstream with the current, then swept round past the gravel bank and leapt towards the low fall at the head of the pool. Each time Alasdair shot out a hand and forced the rod point down; if the line had stayed taut the weight of the falling fish would have snapped the rod like a rotten stick. The sweat dripped from Hakonson's face as he wound and re-wound the reel, only to see the salmon tear back the painfully gained yards of line.

A minute the pound, the experts said. After twenty minutes the fish was still in command. High above on the road the cow was trumpeting its disapproval. Alasdair wiped the midges away from his forehead and stared at the water.

At last the pace began to slacken. The salmon stopped jumping; now he lay deep, head to the current, sulking.

"Reel up," Alasdair ordered Hakonson. "Put the pressure on. But carefully."

A last flurry, and he saw the gleam of the silver belly. Slowly, reluctantly, the salmon broke water. A good fish, a clean-run fish, not a week from the North Sea; on his gills the sea-lice would still be thick. And a big fish for the upper Blackwater —twelve pounds at the least.

"Where's the gaff?" he asked.

"I haven't got one," Hakonson panted. Alasdair could see his arms trembling from the strain. "Just that net over there."

Alasdair looked. The net was tiny, a thing for brown trout, useless for a salmon. There was nothing for it but to wade. He stripped off his jacket and walked out into the river, feeling the cold of the water trickle through his heavy woollen stockings.

"Let him come down with the current," he said to Hakonson. "Then swing him round past me. Keep the pressure on till I shout, then lower your rod—and quickly."

The salmon was very tired now, but his weight and the stream still strained the rod almost into a half-circle. Slowly

Hakonson pulled him out of the stream and across the flat tail of the pool. Alasdair rolled up his shirt-sleeves and waited. Once, twice, the salmon came near, then veered off into deeper water with a flick of his tail. The third time, defeated, he came on, the relentless pressure from the rod leading him to Alasdair's feet. Alasdair watched the steel-grey back slide slowly past, then bent down. One quick snatch with his right hand, just above the tail, and he had the fish out of the water. Panting, he stumbled ashore and threw it on to the bank.

"The net, quick," he snapped.

Hakonson passed the net over. Three blows with the handle on the heavy upper jaw, and the salmon stopped struggling. This was the worst part of the whole business, Alasdair thought. Hooking the fish, playing the fish, tailing the fish— all these were good. But killing the fish, smashing the life out of it while its gills drowned in the empty air—that was different.

He detached the tiny fly from the salmon's throat, slid two fingers through the gills, and stood up, feeling the dead weight heavy on his arm. Now, he told himself, I have killed a fish for a murderer.

"There's your salmon. A cock fish and——"

He broke off. Hakonson was looking past him, his face white.

Alasdair turned. Three feet behind him Ann Wynrame was kneeling in the bracken. She paid no attention to him. Her eyes were fixed on Hakonson, and the grey pistol in her right hand was pointing straight at the American.

Alasdair swung the salmon forward. The great tail, still wet and glistening, caught the pistol and knocked it sideways. He felt the hard bones of the salmon's jaw cut into his fingers. He jumped forward, put his foot on the gun, and stood facing Ann, who was sprawling in the bracken, her face full of a shocked disbelief. He loosened his fingers, and the salmon slid to the ground.

"There's been enough killing," he said in a flat voice. Nobody else spoke.

Out of the corner of his eye he saw figures moving up by the bridge. The guards had spotted what was happening. The realisation stabbed him into action.

He hauled Ann to her feet.

"Run," he said. "You can get away if you move quickly."

She shook her head slowly, surfacing with infinite pain.

"He killed my father," she whispered.

"I know that. Go on. Run."

Her eyes widened. Behind his shoulder he could hear Hakonson panting. Up at the bridge the cow was bellowing. He didn't turn round. And still Ann stayed motionless.

"Go on," he shouted. "Run. If you want to get back to Russia, run, run, run."

"No need to run." Wynrame's voice came from the bank above him. "She can get back to Russia without that. In fact, she hasn't any option."

CHAPTER TWELVE

T H E back of the truck was hard and dirty, and it smelt of cow.
Alasdair could do nothing to hold himself steady, for his hands
were tied behind his back. The pressure of Hakonson's
shoulder didn't help, as the American swayed helplessly from
side to side, his head slumped on his chest. Beyond Hakonson
he could glimpse Ann's hair; she kept her face carefully turned
away from him. Through the cloud of dust that followed them
up the hillside he could see the evicted cow lumbering slowly
towards the river. Then they were over the crest of the hill,
and the view disappeared.

A mile on the Corrachan side of the ridge Wynrame pulled
up, just beyond a flat wooden bridge across a shallow burn.
Igor jumped out, laid something flat and black under the
timbers, and raced back to the truck. Wynrame slammed into
bottom gear and accelerated fiercely. When they were two
hundred yards away there was a small, apologetic explosion,
and the bridge disintegrated. By the time they had reached
Corrachan the operation had been twice repeated. Any pursuing car would have a difficult passage.

In the silence when Wynrame had switched off Alasdair could
hear low voices in the cab. Then Igor came into view at the
tailboard, pistol in hand.

"Get down," he ordered. At close quarters, he was nothing
like a native; it was impossible to mistake him for a keeper or
a shepherd, though he had the correct clothes. His face was
tired. Only his narrow eyes were alert and vicious as he watched
the captives.

"Get down," he repeated, unfastening the tailboard.

Alasdair tried to rise, but his feet slipped on the metal floor
of the truck. There was nothing for it but to wriggle forwards

M

until he could drop to the ground. He swayed with agony as he straightened himself up, his thighs numb from the pounding of the road.

"Down, damn you." Igor was on the point of losing control.

Hakonson, his face pale and his eyes uneasy, followed Alasdair. When Ann reached the ground she glanced quickly at Alasdair, then looked away. He opened his mouth to speak, but thought better of it when Igor swung the pistol round towards him. Nerves were too close to snapping-point for any risks to be taken.

Wynrame appeared beside Igor. He had put his pistol away, and was carrying the Mannlicher stalking-rifle. Noticing Alasdair's glance, he grinned narrowly.

"Yes. The gun itself, Macvartney. I made a mistake when I took it on Friday. But not this time."

He took a box from his pocket, opened the magazine, and slid five bullets in.

"Now, down to the jetty. You're going to row us up the loch. Hurry," he said.

"I'm not," replied Alasdair. "The boat isn't here."

Wynrame's face darkened.

"Where is it?"

"At the head of the loch. I left it there yesterday."

"Why?"

"Because I broke an oar—on your petrol drums."

Too late, Alasdair cursed himself. He had given away too much. Inevitably Wynrame would suspect that Gruar also knew about the petrol. The spy wasn't to know that Gruar had made the wrong decisions. Instead, he would hurry—and every minute was important now. The longer Wynrame took, the more chance there was of saving Ann from what lay ahead. What that was he didn't know: return to Moscow—but after that, what? And now he was entirely on his own. It was too late for anyone else to help.

Wynrame was looking at his watch. The absence of the boat clearly disconcerted him. Igor said something in Russian. Wynrame answered briefly, brusquely.

"You're a damned nuisance, Macvartney," he said, in English. "That means a walk. You'll have to come. I can't offer you a trip to Russia with these two others, but you can lead the way round the loch."

He turned on his heel, went into the lodge, and reappeared with a rope. Loosening the prisoners' hands, he tethered them along the length of the rope—a file of captives on their way to a slave ship, Alasdair thought wryly. As Wynrame tightened the knots, he looked up at the sky. The sun was lipping the ridge of Creag an Lochain; its rays had a flat, elusive quality that made Alasdair catch his breath. But there was little time to watch. A word from Wynrame, and they were moving off towards the suspension bridge over the Blackwater.

The loch was two miles long, and the walk, in normal conditions, would have taken less than an hour. But the cavalcade was slow. The rope hampered quick walking, and only Alasdair and Wynrame of the five were accustomed to the country. At the head of the rope Alasdair soon slipped into a rhythmic stride, checked only by Hakonson's frequent stumbles. He couldn't see Ann; she was at the rear, with Igor, pistol ready, plodding close behind her. Wynrame strode ahead of the procession, at once apprehensive and confident. He was about to bring off a major coup, a victory in an undeclared war, and the nearness of success was intoxicating. Yet things could go wrong, even at this eleventh hour, and the spy remained watchful. Alasdair could see no chance to do anything. He had been right, Gruar had been wrong; but in less than an hour it would be dark, and Ann would be on her way to Russia.

Beyond the bridge the path moved through knee-deep heather, brittle and dry from the heat. At every step clouds of midges were dusted into the air. The wind had fallen at ground level, though the dark clouds were climbing higher and higher. The sun was almost submerged now; as Alasdair watched, the clouds closed in, then washed over it. He moved along mechanically; he was emotionally drained, and his mind took little advantage of its opportunities. He had started back to Corrachan in the hope of stopping Ann going to Russia. Put like that, the intention had been laughable. But what he had found had been something very different. She was going back to Russia, yes; but she was going back under compulsion. Because she had tried to shoot Hakonson, her own side had made her a prisoner, and at once his own chances of success had both increased and diminished. It wasn't a question now of persuading her to change her mind. It was a question of escape —but escape when all the cards were stacked the wrong way.

They came out of a straggling birch wood and rounded a promontory. Ahead, less than a mile away, the golden sands glimmered in the fading light. Time was running out. Out on the loch the trout were rising to the evening hatch of flies, their incessant dimpling breaking the smooth mirror of the water.

"Is your friend Gruar looking for us?" Wynrame said suddenly, his voice harsh in the stillness.

"Of course. He's no fool," Alasdair replied shortly.

"Agreed. But is he looking for us here?"

"I don't know." It was the best Alasdair could do. "What I do know is that your ship has been spotted."

Wynrame laughed.

"I hoped it would be. A clever man, Mr. Gruar. But not clever enough. He'll have planes waiting for us, I suppose. So it's a pity that we're not going to any ship that he can see. We're being picked up by a helicopter from the ship, yes, but it's going to take us south, not north. There's a submarine waiting off the mouth of Rhintraid Bay, and I don't think Mr. Gruar will be expecting that. I only hope this American won't spend his time being seasick all the way to Murmansk."

Now that he knew the whole plan, Alasdair's depression increased. Not only had Gruar failed to stop the Corrachan bolt-hole; he had been even more thoroughly out-thought over the escape route. To fly in a helicopter, refuel it on Loch Skiag, then make a get-away in exactly the opposite direction, was outside Gruar's calculations. There was no question of the escape being stopped now. Channel Z had been opened successfully.

And Hakonson? He shot a glance over his shoulder at the American.

Wynrame saw him, and laughed again.

"Yes, he's coming too. That wasn't my idea. I never liked it, and I told my bosses so. When they had wind from America that he was coming here they got too greedy—and too clever. They wanted to collect him, so they sent over a man who could listen in to the conference and who could put pressure on Hakonson too——"

"His brother," Alasdair said.

"Exactly. I thought Gruar would ferret that out. It wasn't a very good plan. They hadn't remembered that Hakonson had stolen his brother's wife. They didn't reckon on the two meeting at the Craggan garage on Friday night, before we were properly organised. They didn't reckon on Hakonson knocking his brother unconscious and dumping him in the river. And they should never have risked sending the man here at all, when his daughter was already on the spot. In fact, the whole business was so crazy that I can only imagine someone at headquarters thought it was a good idea. That would cheer Gruar up. We've got our fools too. It was a bungled piece of work—not professional at all."

Wynrame was more talkative than Alasdair had ever heard him before. Absurdly, he was reminded of Gruar. It was the word 'professional' that did it. Wynrame and Gruar were two of a kind, playing their own secret game with its own secret rules. For a moment the whole business shrank, lost magnitude. Then he remembered Thomson, and the agent who had been killed keeping watch at Cornessie. And now Ann was going back to Russia. After this night he would never see her again.

"What about your wife?" He had to ask the question.

Wynrame snapped off a rush-stem and began to chew it. They had gone another hundred yards before he replied.

"Quite simple. She wanted to shoot her uncle. Nothing to blame her for in that, but it wasn't what was ordered. We were told to get Hakonson and ship him to Russia. I wouldn't be very popular if I brought a corpse with me. If you like, it's all my bosses' fault. They sent her here in the first place because her mother was Scottish, but they should have kept her out of the way when this operation was planned. These family complications never help our business. However, you stopped her killing Hakonson, which was good of you—some compensation for seducing her and getting in our way earlier on. Thanks to you, I can deliver Hakonson as requested, and she can do her own explaining when we get home. So I can follow my inclinations and leave you alive. Igor, now, wouldn't be quite so lenient."

Alasdair said nothing. The whole situation was clear now. Gruar's miscalculations—every one of them understandable —fell into place. He had been worried about Dounreay, he had considered the danger of the conference being tapped, but he had never thought of kidnapping. Yet the situation was an ideal one; in a matter of hours Hakonson could be beyond recall. The first and crucial mistake once made, the later ones only underlined where the advantage lay. Wynrame could afford to talk, could afford to leave him contemptuously alive. The game was won and lost.

"If you're wondering why I'm being generous," Wynrame said, throwing the rush away, "let me say that she isn't my wife in any sense of the word. She's simply been a good agent to work with. She helped on Friday night, when I suspected that you were the killer. You might have recognised me in the woods, if she hadn't turned the charm on you. She also got the vital clue out of you that gave Hakonson away. Then she had to go and get involved with you, which was a waste, but at least gave me the chance to search your cottage. So I'm not playing the injured husband—but I'm not getting myself into trouble because of her. She's coming back to stand the racket herself."

They came out on the edge of the sands. The night-moths were beginning to stir. Somewhere back in the birches a hunting owl called twice. Soon it would be too dark to make out where the water ended and the hill began. Already Creag an Lochain was a vast black menace, merging into the banked-up clouds.

Wynrame knew where he was going. Half-way along the

shore he stopped, and motioned to the slave-train to halt. Alasdair obeyed thankfully; Hakonson dropped on to his knees; only Ann stood upright, staring into an unguessable distance. Wynrame drew a torch from his pocket and searched in the long grass beyond the sand. With a grunt of satisfaction he found what he was hunting, and came back towards them, pulling a thin wire out of the sand as he walked. He followed it down to the water, then tugged sharply. There was a gurgle, a splash on the face of the loch, and something black spun and rolled in the half-light. Alasdair knew what was there. The fuel drums were floating on the surface.

Igor looked at his watch and spoke in Russian. Wynrame nodded, cocking his head on one side. A trout splashed, the owl called again—and then there came a faint humming noise, far away and high above. It grew quickly, bounced and bounced again from the cliffs of Creag an Lochain, then moved nearer. Wynrame took the torch from his pocket and flashed it thrice into the sky. Somewhere above another light replied. The humming noise changed into a drone, then into a roar. A dark and monstrous shape fell out of the sky and hovered above the water, lashing it into white foam. Wynrame shone his torch again, and inch by inch the monster dropped downwards, till it touched the loch. The roaring stopped, and the sound of the waves slapping against the sand took its place. Then there was silence once again, and the helicopter rocked gently beside the drums.

A hatch slid back, a head appeared in silhouette, and a voice called to the shore. Wynrame replied, then went some twenty yards along the sands. He untied the boat that Alasdair had abandoned, pushed off, and punted out to the helicopter. There were scraping noises, the sound of a stopper being unscrewed, and from inside the machine a hose was passed out. Wynrame fastened it to one of the barrels, and came quickly back to the shore. He climbed out, untied the rope which joined the three prisoners, and gestured to Igor.

"Tie Macvartney's wrists, get the other two out to the helicopter, and then come back for me. I'll cover you from here."

Igor nodded, bound Alasdair's hands savagely with cord, and turned to Hakonson. The American staggered to his feet in response to a kick and looked round, his eyes sick and scared. He started to run away, his legs floundering in the soft sand. Within a few paces Igor was beside him and hit him once over the temple with the butt of his revolver. The scientist crumpled forward and lay still. Wynrame watched impassively as Igor picked him up and slid him into the boat.

When Igor had straightened up Wynrame motioned to Ann to get in also. She took two steps, then turned suddenly and looked straight at Alasdair.

"I'm sorry," she said. Something passed between them, but so swiftly and so comprehensively that when it was past Alasdair could not remember everything that it had contained.

Ann began to speak quickly. Igor lifted a hand, but Wynrame waved him down.

"It's never as simple as you think." She was struggling in desperate haste to find the words. "I'm not frightened of going back. The people in the strath are kind, but I've met others just as kind in Russia. I'm not sorry that I tried to kill that man. He broke my father's heart and made him cold and hard and bitter. I'm not sorry for anything, except——"

Her voice tailed away.

Something told Alasdair to be very careful. He waited.

Then she smiled uncertainly.

"Except," she went on, "except that I wasn't honest with you. I knew that it mattered as soon as you kissed me, and then it was too late. I'm not frightened, but I don't want to go back, because now you will never know what I really am."

Alasdair smiled back at her. There was a numb hopelessness inside him, but he forced himself to smile.

"I know enough to be going on with. We're not beaten yet."

She shook her head slowly.

"No," she said. "We are beaten."

"That's enough," said Wynrame. "Get into the boat."

Ann climbed in and sat down, her feet hard against the unconscious Hakonson. Igor took the only oar and poled his way out to the helicopter, Wynrame watching like a cat all the time. A ladder slid down, and Ann was forced to climb into the machine. A rope followed, and Hakonson's body was hoisted up. Then the boat made for the shore again.

When it landed, Wynrame got in and stood in the bows. Igor sat in the stern and pulled out his revolver. Wynrame emptied the magazine of the Mannlicher and tossed the bullets into the water one by one.

"I'm going to cut your rope in a few minutes, Macvartney," he said. "Then you can go back to that damned strath and the cattle who live in it. I've had my bellyful of them. They didn't accept me and they won't accept you, but back you go and crawl to them. I'm going home. You can put that rifle back in the gun-room at Craggan. I'm not a thief."

A voice called urgently from the helicopter. Wynrame swung round. Alasdair followed his gaze. Far away, on the slope above Corrachan, lights were moving.

"We're leaving now," Wynrame said to Alasdair. "Here comes your friend Gruar—too late as usual. Turn round."

Alasdair turned. He felt the cord being sliced away from his wrists, then he was pushed violently forwards. He fell on his face in the sand. By the time he was on his feet again the boat was at the helicopter, and the two men were scrambling aboard. The ladder was hauled in, a hand waved mockingly from the open hatch, and was gone. A cough, a splutter, and then a steady roar as the engine fired. The helicopter rocked on the water, the blast from the rotor driving the boat broadside on to the beach. Then the machine was in the air, lifting slowly.

A drop of rain fell on Alasdair's hand. The storm was about to break. He rubbed the back of his hand against his jacket, and struck something hard through the tweed. It was a bullet. Two bullets. Five bullets—the five bullets from the Corrachan Mannlicher that he had stuffed in his pocket the afternoon before, when Cattanach had found him with Erica. Five bullets—and there was another Mannlicher less than ten yards away, lying in the empty boat where Wynrame had left it.

It took him a second to realise the implications. Already the helicopter was fifty yards away, climbing every instant, gaining height before wheeling west to skirt the face of the mountain. In a very short time it would be out of range. And Ann was a helpless passenger in it.

He hesitated, then ran to the boat. The rain was getting heavier and a surly wind was growling through it. He stuffed the bullets into the rifle. The helicopter, veering in the grip of a current from the rocks, swung round, and the lighted cockpit came into his sights. He took aim, estimated the range automatically, and fired three times. The machine leapt in the air, the rotor racing frantically, hung on a point of time, then swooped drunkenly forwards and upwards into the face of Creag an Lochain. There was a crack, a dull thud, a long scraping roar—and a pinpoint of red light against the blackness of the mountain.

He ran headlong across the sands, splashing in the shallows to get a firmer foothold. The sand hardened, gave way to stones, then to rocks, and the light flickered into a blaze. He was going to be too late, too late to undo what he had done. A startled bird flapped in his face, screeched and disappeared. He could feel the heat of the fire. And then he was amongst the wreckage, shielding his face from the glare, searching desperately for a girl with black hair.

All at once he found her. She was lying face downwards across a splintered seat, blood running down the side of her head. He grabbed her under the arms and pulled frantically. The wreckage gave way and she tumbled on to the rocks. Picking her up, he ran down the hillside, plunging from boulder to boulder, till his feet slipped and he rolled, still clutching her, into the water. Behind him there came a roar, a gust of hot air, and a long throbbing hiss. He ducked under water and pulled Ann with him. Around them debris spattered the loch, hissing and glowing as it fell. And then there was silence.

*   *   *

An age later he was carrying her along the sands through

the darkness. The rain was falling steadily, the sky was black, and the wind was rising second by second. Ahead he could see the boat swinging uneasily from side to side. At any moment it might drift out of the shelter of the shore, and then the wind would take it and send it down the loch. More than anything else he wanted to catch the boat before it went out of his reach. He was soaked to the skin, his hands were scorched, and he was more tired than he had ever been before. To have to walk the two miles back round the shore was an unendurable thought. He wanted the boat. He would lay Ann on the floor-boards, where Hakonson had been thrown, and they would drift with the wind, gliding past the points and the bays, back to Corrachan through the white-topped waves. What he would do after that he didn't know, didn't care. She was alive, he knew, for her heart was beating, but she was still unconscious. And he was alive. And up on the edge of the mountain were four dead men. But he could think of nothing but the boat.

It was just out of his reach, so he waded up to his waist to clutch the trailing bow-rope. The wind drove at the boat, pulling it away from him, but he leaned on the rope, and slowly hauled it in. The keel grounded with a hiss, and he let the rope drop, holding on to the side of the boat to get his breath back. He looked at Ann where she lay on the sand. She was stirring, moaning softly as she did so. He dropped to his knees, pulled his jacket off, and slipped it round her shoulders. She opened her eyes, and he saw recognition in them. He bent down and kissed her eyes. She tried to smile, shivered, and relaxed again; her eyes closed.

He stood up, felt automatically in his pockets for a cigarette, then realised that any that he had would be ruined by the water. One of his wrists still ached from being tied; he rubbed at it while he stood, trying to organise his thoughts, trying to drive himself to pick Ann up and carry her to the boat. His body was being obstinate, perverse, refusing to obey. To get into the boat meant to go back to Corrachan, to go back to the world outside, and the effort was not to be thought of. He looked back at the wreck, where the wind was still whipping up a few glowing embers into an occasional flame. There was nobody else alive there; and he didn't feel sorry.

A light came out of the grass and flooded round him, leaving deep pools of darkness on Ann's face and in the lee of the boat. He cowered from the light, hating it and all that it stood for. The world outside had not waited for him; it had come to find him.

Gruar's voice came out of the rain.

"Well, Alasdair, you can't keep out of it, can you?"

"If you did your job better, I might be able to," Alasdair retorted, the ashes of anger reddening inside him.

"Possibly. You've lost the Air Force an interesting job. And you may have found yourself another one. We must have a look at Mrs. Wynrame—and you're hurt yourself, too."

Men came out of the night into the torchlight. One bent over Ann with a first-aid kit. Another brought blankets and laid them in the boat. Gruar himself appeared, inevitable cigarette packet in his hand. Alasdair accepted one gratefully, and allowed his hands to be dressed and bandaged.

"What happened?" said Gruar, when the bandaging was finished.

Alasdair told him. The agent said nothing, but went across to where the rifle was lying and picked it up. He balanced it in one hand, and turned to look at Alasdair.

"You know, you're rather a remarkable man," he said. "Not many men would have been able to do that."

Alasdair was embarrassed. Any stalker worth his salt would have taken one shot only, not three. He turned the subject away.

"How did you spot that they had come here?" he asked.

"I never ruled it out, you know, though I should have paid more attention to what you said. The two guards at the bridge weren't very clever; we found them both knocked out and tied up under the arch. But then Wynrame wasn't very clever either. He should never have let your cow loose. She turned up at the farm about an hour after you had left, and old Jardine, who's quite an admirer of yours, realised something had happened.

Sensibly, he got in touch with me, and we came up to Corrachan."

The man with the first-aid kit came across and spoke to Gruar.

"The woman's all right. That cut on her head is superficial, and she's got some burns, but apart from that it's just shock. We must get her back to some warmth as soon as possible."

Gruar looked at Alasdair.

"Anything more to tell me?" he asked.

"She's Hakonson's niece all right, and the dead man was her father. Hakonson killed him, so she tried to shoot Hakonson on the river this afternoon. I got in the way, and then Wynrame and Igor turned up and collected us all. She was on her way back to Russia to explain why she had exceeded her instructions."

"I see." Gruar was silent for a long time. Men were lifting Ann, wrapping her in blankets, laying her under a raincoat in the stern of the boat. Alasdair watched. She had led him on, she had been a spy, she had tried to kill her own uncle. But he had kissed her, suspecting much of what he now knew; and he had saved her from death by fire, knowing everything.

"What will happen to her?" he asked Gruar.

"That rather depends on you, doesn't it? We've nothing positive against her, unless you make a statement."

"And if I don't?"

"Then there is nothing to stop her going on living in this country. Her papers are in as perfect order as you would expect any Russian agent's to be. Of course, we would be interested if she cared to give us a little information about her past friends."

Alasdair looked straight at him.

"I'm going to marry her," he said. "And you can be quite clear about one thing. I'm not acting as your spy, and I'm not going to let you make her an informer."

"Right. I'll accept that. But just remember one or two things yourself, Alasdair. I don't do this job because I think it's morally defensible, or because I like power or glory or anything

like that. I do it because I can do it well, and because a lot
of people would suffer if it wasn't done at all. I very nearly
made a mess of this particular assignment, and it's no thanks
to myself that I didn't. You needn't imagine that I enjoy saying
this, but it's true. You did the real work this time; I guessed
wrong, you guessed right, and then you broke the whole thing
wide open by yourself. I owe you something for that."

"What are you going to do, then? I won't let you hurt her."

"I'm going to do this," Gruar said. "There's going to be no
public mention of the helicopter or the crash. I'll have to make
my report, of course, but only half a dozen people will ever see
it. We'll clean up the mess here—dump the wreckage in the
loch, and get rid of the bodies. All the story that need get back
is that Wynrame and Hakonson came up here to look around,
and were drowned while out rowing. Cattanach will keep his
mouth shut. He may get enough of a case against Hakonson to
put in a report, but the Procurator-Fiscal can't prosecute a dead
man. Channel Z is closed, officially, and you can do what you
like."

"I'm staying in the strath," Alasdair said.

"Good. I hoped you would. This is where you belong. Now
I'll row you back to Corrachan. We brought a pair of spare
oars, for I knew you had broken one here. But we'll empty
this flask first."

Alasdair drank his share and climbed into the boat, shivering
with the heat of the whisky. Gruar took the oars and pushed
off. The rain was slackening, and the wind was falling away.
The warm south-west air struck softly round their faces, and
far above he could see the Ploughman driving his furrow across
a gap in the clouds. He looked down at Ann. She was awake
again, looking gravely up at him. He didn't smile. There was
too much to remember, too much to anticipate.

The loch was quietening. Already they were well out from
the sands, and the waters were stretching all around them. He
lifted his head and looked at Gruar. The bargain had been
struck, the account had been balanced. Gruar rested on his
oars, leaned down, picked something up, and handed it to him.

It was the Mannlicher. Alasdair took it in his hands and stood up. Gruar nodded. Alasdair threw the rifle as far as he could into the loch. No Excalibur, this. No hand reached up to catch it. But a running salmon leapt and splashed through the widening ripples. Gruar rowed on. Alasdair watched the ripples die, turning to see them as the boat moved forwards. Then he looked at Ann, and settled down in his seat to wait.

For regular early information

about

FORTHCOMING NOVELS

send a postcard

giving your name and address

in block capitals

to

THE FICTION EDITOR

HODDER & STOUGHTON LTD.,
St. Paul's House, Warwick Square,
London, E.C.4.